WOODLAND WEB

MOONSHADOW BAY
BOOK 12

YASMINE GALENORN

A Nightqueen Enterprises LLC Publication

Published by Yasmine Galenorn

PO Box 2037, Kirkland WA 98083-2037

WOODLAND WEB

A Moonshadow Bay Novella

Copyright © 2024 by Yasmine Galenorn

First Electronic Printing: 2024 Nightqueen Enterprises LLC

First Print Edition: 2024 Nightqueen Enterprises

Cover Art & Design: Ravven

Art Copyright: Yasmine Galenorn

Editor: Elizabeth Flynn

A Nightqueen Enterprises LLC Publication

Published in the United States of America

ACKNOWLEDGMENTS

Thanks to my usual crew: Samwise, my husband, Andria, and Jennifer. Without their help, I'd be swamped. To the women who have helped me find my way in indie, you're all great, and thank you to everyone. To my wonderful cover artist, Ravven, for the beautiful work she's done, and to my editor, Elizabeth, who helps me keep my ellipses under control—thank you both.

Also, my love to my furbles, who keep me happy. My most reverent devotion to Mielikki, Tapio, Ukko, Rauni, and Brighid, my spiritual guardians and guides. My love and reverence to Herne, and Cernunnos, and to the Fae, who still rule the wild places of this world. And a nod to the Wild Hunt, which runs deep in my magick, as well as in my fiction.

You can find me through my website at Galenorn.com and be sure to sign up for my newsletter to keep updated on all my latest releases! You can find my advice on writing, discussions about the books, and general ramblings on my YouTube channel. If you liked this book, I'd be grateful if you'd leave a review—it helps more than you can think.

May 2024
Brightest Blessings,
-The Painted Panther-
-Yasmine Galenorn-

WELCOME TO WOODLAND WEB

Finally, the shadow man is gone. I've been on sabbatical, trying to work on a book, but I'm getting antsy to return to my job. And then, one beautiful April morning, Rebecca the imp delivers a message to me: Briar, the Fae Lord who helped us when we were trying to save Tad and Hank from Bigfoot, has called in my debt. It's time to repay the favor.

A dangerous member of the sub-Fae has escaped from the Overking's realm and it's loose in Moonshadow Bay. If the Court Magika discovers that a sluagh is running around, it could endanger negotiations between the witchblood and the Fae. So Briar assigns the task to me: find and destroy the sluagh. The trouble is, I can't tell my grandmother about it, or *any* member of the Court.

So it's back to Conjure Ink to resume work on a part-time basis, and to enlist the agency's help in tracking down the sub-Fae. Can I manage to clear my debt to the Overkings? And can we destroy the sluagh before it goes on a killing spree through Moonshadow Bay?

CHAPTER ONE

I STARED OUT OF THE WINDOW, THINKING HOW ODD IT WAS
that I didn't have to get up to go to work. I was on a sabbatical still, but getting bored enough to realize that I probably should go back to work. I wasn't happy when I wasn't busy, and even though I had more time now to learn the magic I needed to learn and to spend with my grandmother and aunt, I couldn't—and didn't—expect them to spend every moment of every day holding my hand. But I had figured out that I was an extrovert at heart, and I missed seeing my friends and coworkers every day.

I turned over and gently prodded Killian. "Hey, wake up. It's morning. It's seven."

He grunted, snored once, then turned over.

I prodded him again, a little harder. "It's time to get up and go to work," I said. Then I leaned close and began nuzzling his ear and neck. "Do you know what you're missing by sleeping? Get up now and we might have time for—"

That was all it took. Killian blinked, turning over to yawn and stare at me with hungry eyes.

"I'm awake," he said, lifting the covers so I could see that, yes, he was definitely awake. All parts of him.

"You should get up and shower—"

He snorted, pulling me into his arms. "Oh no, woman. You tease me like that, you have to at least kiss me."

I melted into his arms, my boredom forgotten. He was warm against my side and his lust was hard to ignore. *So hard. So...very...*hard.

"You're making this difficult," I whispered, pressing my breasts against his chest. Morning sex was good. I loved morning sex—it was a flurry of warmth and coziness and that hope that only comes early in the day when everything else felt like a blur, still. "I'd love to make love, but... Last night you asked me to remind you that it's your low-income spay and neuter day at the clinic."

Killian was a veterinarian, and he and the other vets in town had divided up the months into two categories. Each month, half of the vets would hold a free spay and neuter day for low-income clients. The other half would offer low-cost appointments for vaccinations and overall wellness checks. The next month, they swapped out for the other category.

There were six other vets in town, and Killian had quickly risen to the top in popularity. That meant he was able to spearhead his favorite projects. This—the free care for low-income customers and their pets—meant the world to him. But the clinics were long, from early morning until night, and the sooner he got to the office, the better.

"Woman, you'd kick me out of bed just to send me to work?" He stretched and kissed me again. Before I could protest, he sighed. "You're right. I'll shower. Make us some breakfast?"

I nodded. "I'll drag my ass out of bed to make breakfast, yes." As I slid into my robe and slippers, Killian padded naked into the bathroom. He was a fine sight, front and back.

Xi and Klaus stirred, jumped off the bed, and led me into the kitchen. Generally, Killian and I took turns making breakfast. When I had a migraine, he would cook for me, when I could eat. When I was at work, we took turns cooking. But since I'd gone on sabbatical, I had taken over most of the cooking, since I had the time.

As I whipped up eggs for omelets and popped bread in the toaster, my phone rang. I glanced at the clock. I reached for the phone and saw that it was Meagan. Surprised—I hadn't heard from Ari's wife since Ari and I had fallen out, plus it was awfully early for a phone call—I turned the heat down and answered.

"Hey," I said, hesitant. I didn't know why she called, and I wasn't sure how to respond.

"Hey," Meagan said. "Listen, I know you must be surprised to hear from me, but can we meet for coffee today?"

At least she didn't sound angry.

I took a deep breath, deciding that meeting her couldn't hurt. It wasn't like I'd been bothering Ari. We'd talked a couple times, but we still were circling the outskirts of our old friendship, and neither one of us were sure what to do next. I desperately missed my former best friend, but I wasn't about to push her with an ultimatum. Plus, if we couldn't be friends again, I wasn't ready to hear it. So I'd kept away, honoring her request, hoping for something to heal the rift.

"Sure," I said. "I can do that. Where and when?"

"Ten, at Jerry's?"

Jerry's was a new coffee shop that had recently opened on the other side of town, away from both Ari and Meagan's house and away from my house. I had a sneaking suspicion that Ari didn't know that Meagan was talking to me. But it seemed prudent to clarify matters.

"Does Ari know we're meeting?"

Meagan paused for a moment, then said, "No, actually, she

doesn't. But if she asked, I'd tell her. Trust me, this is aboveboard—"

"I wouldn't expect anything less of you," I said. "Okay, ten A.M., at Jerry's." As I went back to cooking, I wondered what Meagan wanted to talk about.

AT TEN A.M. PROMPTLY, I WAS SITTING IN JERRY'S, SIPPING on a triple-shot iced latte, eating a doughnut. I had given up sugar, for the most part because it aggravated my energy reflux syndrome, but now and then I let myself have a treat, and today I definitely needed it. I wasn't sure what Meagan was going to say, and I decided I wasn't about to beat myself up over eating a couple pastries to calm my nerves.

Every time the door opened, I glanced up. I wasn't sure why I was so worried—it wasn't like Meagan could make the situation worse—but for some reason, I felt a little guilty. The argument hadn't been my fault, nor had it really been Ari's fault. It was situational, and there had been no way for us to avoid it. But it all came down to my occupation and how Ari thought I was too dangerous to be around their adopted children.

A few moments later, Meagan came in. The first thing I noticed was she had cut her hair. It was in a short, cute bob now, and it suited her. The second was that she looked vaguely like the cat that ate the canary. Or the bear...given Meagan was a bear shifter.

"Hey, what's up?" I asked as she slid into the chair opposite me.

She glanced at the counter. "Let me get some caffeine. I'm going to need it."

I watched as she approached the barista and gave him her order, then returned to the table. "He'll bring it over. Thanks for meeting me today." She frowned. "I'm not sure that, if I were you, I would have agreed. So I appreciate it."

Surprised to hear her say that, I shrugged. "Why wouldn't I?"

Even as I said it, I realized that Ari's decision still stung. I still hurt from her panic that I might put her children in danger. But I couldn't refute that hanging around with me actually might be dangerous, and even that *sliver* of possibility made me feel guilty, though I'd never willingly put them in harm's way.

"So...how *are* you? How's Killian doing?"

Hearing Meagan struggle to make small talk was worse than ripping off the bandage. Meagan was no-nonsense, and she had always left the gossip to Ari and me.

"You know, why don't you just say what you came to say? It's not that I don't appreciate the attempt, but obviously, you're here for a reason. If Ari doesn't know you're here, then she'd probably be angry to find out you are. What's going on, Meagan?" I was still enough of an emotional wreck from the fight that I couldn't be any more tactful than that.

Meagan paused as the barista brought over her mocha and a sandwich. As soon as the server left the table, she turned to me, sighing again. "Okay, you want to know why I'm here, I'll tell you. I can't stand this fight between you and Ari a moment longer. She's miserable, and she mopes all day. The kids know something's wrong, and I'm about to go off on her. It was a stupid fight, so I want you both to make up."

She sat back, mocha in hand, staring at me.

I blinked. "What? I thought you were coming down here to tell me that you wanted me to stay far away from your family."

Meagan snorted. "Okay, here's the thing. First, just *living* in this town puts everyone in danger, but it wouldn't be different anywhere else. There are always going to be dangers

5

around, especially for those of us in the Otherkin community. Second, Ari's witchblood like you. That alone can attract the things she's afraid of. She just freaked out when that demon possessed her—as anybody would. But it could have happened anywhere. You're not directly responsible. There's nothing special about you, January, that makes you more of a threat."

I wasn't sure whether to be insulted or flattered.

"And third," she continued, "Ari needs her bestie. I love her, but she's my wife. You're her lifelong best friend, and nothing can replace that. I don't want to sit and gossip. I don't know how to talk about magic. I don't care if High Priestess Floofernuts demands that Ari return to the coven—no offense to your grandmother, by the way. I just want to love her, eat dinner with her and the kids at night, and see that they're all happy. And Ari's terribly unhappy right now."

I nodded, realizing that Meagan hadn't been instrumental in Ari's decision. "Did you tell her that?"

Meagan blinked. "No...she knows all that."

"Maybe she doesn't know as much as you think she does. You do realize that she thought this is what *you* wanted? That you'd be so terrified for the kids that you'd welcome her kicking me out of her life. She didn't exactly say that, but I've known Ari for decades, now, and trust me, that's what she was thinking."

"You have to be kidding," Meagan said.

"Most definitely not. And there's something else you may not realize. Ari's petrified by the sudden responsibility of caring for two children that she never expected to show up on her doorstep. She wants to do right by them." I leaned forward, suddenly grateful that I'd given Meagan the chance to talk to me. "Ari's afraid she'll hurt them, somehow. And when that demon possessed her and she was headed back to the salon where the kids were..."

CHAPTER TWO

An hour later, invested with a jury-rigged plan, I headed for the grocery store.

I was halfway through shopping when I realized I was bored. I'd been off work for a couple of months. I had started writing a book about my experiences, but at heart, I preferred writing articles. I thought about starting a blog, which I was still playing around with, but that wouldn't take up all my time. And I wasn't geared to be a housewife.

My phone alerted me and I paused in the baking aisle to see who was texting me. It was Tally, my sister-in-law.

Since Ari had turned her back on me, Tally and I'd grown closer. At first, I thought I might be trying to prove that I was safe to be around with if you had children, but Tally and I had always gotten along, and the longer we hung out, the closer we were growing. I genuinely enjoyed spending time with her. She wasn't my BFF, not like Ari had been, but we had formed a comfortable friendship over the past few months. That made Killian happy, too, so it was a win-win-win situation.

January, do you and Killian still want to get

TOGETHER FOR GAME NIGHT? I NEED TO KNOW SO I CAN
CALL A BABYSITTER.

WHY HIRE A BABYSITTER? BRING THE TWINS WITH YOU.
KILLIAN LOVES HIS NIECES TO PIECES. HA, THERE'S MY INNER
POET COMING OUT. I snorted as I texted back.

YOU KNOW WE LOVE THAT YOU GUYS WATCH VICTORIA
AND LEANNA FOR US, BUT I WANT A NIGHT AWAY FROM THE
BABIES. SO I HATE TO DISAPPOINT YOU, BUT IT'S GOING TO
JUST BE US!

NO PROBLEM. WHAT DO YOU WANT FOR DINNER? I
THOUGHT I MIGHT MAKE LASAGNA.

LES LOVES YOUR COOKING—AND SO DO I. I DON'T CARE
IF WE EAT SHOE LEATHER AS LONG AS I DON'T HAVE TO COOK
IT, BUT LASAGNA SOUNDS FANTASTIC. SEE YOU TOMORROW
NIGHT AT AROUND SEVEN, Talley said.

I grinned at the phone. Tally loved being a mother, but
she wasn't ready to give up her everyday life to play nurse-
maid, and she wanted to find a job outside the house. They
couldn't afford a nanny, though, so when Serena and William
—Killian and Tally's parents—offered to move to Moonshadow Bay to help out with the grandkids, we all pitched in
with house-hunting and found the perfect house for them.
They had just closed on it and moved in. There had been no
difficulties because they had bought my old home and were
now our new neighbors.

"Are you sure you want them next door?" Killian had
asked. "I know you all get along, but..."

"But nothing. They want to be in town to help your
sister, and I hate seeing my house sit empty. I never thought
I'd sell it, but given they agreed to let me make the first offer
if they ever want to sell it, I'm fine." I paused, then added,
"You don't know how good it feels to have family next door,
even if they're technically not my blood. I know I have
Rowan and Aunt Teran, but your parents treat me like one of

their own. They treat me like I matter, and I'm so grateful for that."

"If you don't mind, I think it would be great." Killian had been so happy that I worried it might not work out—that maybe something would happen to disrupt everything. But Serena and William had lived next door for a month now and everything had been fine. Serena was taking a sabbatical from working to watch after the grandchildren, and William had expanded his business. He was an accountant, and while he had lost some of his clients by moving, he had also added a number of new ones.

I slid my phone back in my purse and added a box of lasagna noodles to the cart. I already had the makings for sauce at home, and I just needed more ricotta and some mozzarella. I thought about dessert for a moment and decided on lemon poundcake with a blueberry compote.

After adding a cake mix to the cart—I didn't usually make pound cake and I wanted it to turn out right—I stopped in the frozen foods aisle for berries. We still had a few months till berry season and, after eating the ones grown locally, it was hard to buy imported ones. They always had that leathery feel blueberries get when they were a little too old. So frozen was a good way to go, and would make a delicious compote.

I finished the shopping, then headed home, thinking about Meagan. It didn't surprise me that she was involved in sports—she was the dean of women's sports at a local college —because she was more brawn than brain. Oh, she was smart enough, but her first instincts were to go the blunt, direct route. And that was true of most bear shifters. They were direct and honest, and you knew up front what they wanted from you.

As I arrived home and put away the groceries, I noticed something out back. There was something hanging on the gate that separated the two houses. We'd left the gate up when I agreed to sell, to give some semblance of privacy. I'd also insisted on keeping half the lot—the back half that buttressed the Mystic Wood. Given neither of Killian's parents were only marginally interested in gardening, they had willingly given up the extra quarter acre in exchange for a reduction in price.

I put away the frozen foods then headed outside, squinting as a ray of sunlight hit my eyes. The weather in western Washington dithered in May, sometimes deciding we were on our way to summer, sometimes deciding to return to the blustery chill of spring. Today, we were getting the warmth. I stopped by the side gate where I saw a red sparkling ribbon tied to the post. I knew what that meant.

I glanced back at the house. The stove was off, and the door was shut to keep the cats in, so I untied the ribbon and headed toward the back of the lot. There, a bench sat at the trailhead leading into the Mystic Wood. The woodland sparkled with magic, and odd and sometimes dangerous creatures made their home within the boundaries. In the past few years, I'd come to know the woodland a lot better, but that only made me keep my guard up even more. Not all monsters wore frightening guises, and some of the most charming were more than willing to feed on grown witch women.

But I knew who had left the red ribbon. If it was tied on the gate, it meant Rebecca the imp wanted to talk to me. If I tied it on the bench by the trailhead, it meant I needed to talk to her. That we'd managed to come as far as we had astonished me. I'd always assumed she'd been trying to kill me when I was a child, but recently I'd figured out that she'd been trying to keep me from harm—to keep me safe from darker creatures lurking within the Mystic Woods.

I sat on the bench by the trailhead and waited. A moment later, Rebecca peered out of the thicket. She looked like a golden-haired ten-year-old girl, so perfect that she couldn't be human. Rebecca was a minor demon—an imp—but we'd come to a meeting of the minds and while I wouldn't say we were friends, we were the next best thing. *Allies.*

"Hey, what's up?" We hadn't talked in several weeks, but that wasn't uncommon. Usually, Rebecca contacted me when something odd happened, or if there was danger around. Whenever I got a message that she wanted to see me, I spent my time waiting for the other shoe to drop.

"I have a message for you." She looked so serious that it took me aback. Rebecca usually started with some semblance of small talk—*hello, how are you*, or whatnot. That she dove right in didn't bode well.

"What is it? From whom?" It wasn't like we ran in the same social circles with mutual friends.

"I bear a message from Briar, the Overking."

Briar? Crap. Briar was one of the Overkings, or as we knew them—the Fae. And the Fae were not to be trifled with. They could be cruel and vicious, and the last thing anybody wanted was a run-in with them. And I owed him a favor.

I could feel the color draining out of my face. "What does he want?"

"I don't know—I wasn't about to ask," Rebecca said. She handed me a large envelope that felt like it was made out of handmade paper, like papyrus. It was sealed with some sort of waxen seal to keep it closed. With one look, I could tell that it hadn't been tampered with.

I stared at the envelope in my hand, dreading opening it. "I wonder what would happen if I just ignored it."

Rebecca let out a little hiss. "Don't even think it. The last person you want angry at you is one of the Overkings. They're not even from *my* sphere, but I know better than to cross them. There's a reason the Woodlings don't revolt against their slavery. The Overkings have little in the way of compassion, and they're arrogant because they're so powerful

—not because they just *think* they are." She hesitated, then said, "Do you want me to open it for you?"

I flipped the envelope over. On the front, in a spidery scrawl, it read: Ms. January Jaxson. "I guess...no. I got myself into this situation. It's up to me to deal with the fallout. But can you stay while I open it?"

"Of course," Rebecca said, gingerly sitting on the bench near me. She didn't like being touched.

"Thanks," I said. I took a deep breath, then decided to rip the bandage off. I broke the wax seal and slid the folded pages out of the envelope. As I opened them, the feel of magic surrounded me. The Fae were powerful and they mirrored the energy coming from the Mystic Wood. I scanned the first page, reading the thin, coiling words aloud:

"January: I am calling in your debt. You will attend to this matter to the best of your ability. I need you to keep this quiet—you may ask your friends for help, in fact, I expect you'll need to, but this is not something for public knowledge. You are not to tell your grandmother or any other member of the Court Magika. There are some delicate deliberations taking place between the Overkings and the Court Magika, and this could disrupt the balance of those negotiations.

"One of our sub-Fae has escaped the dungeons. A sluagh is loose in the Mystic Wood, and he's good at hiding. The sluagh is dangerous, and he *must* be destroyed before he begins terrorizing Moonshadow Bay. We attempted to track him, but he's managed to enter your world. This means we can't go about at will to find him, because we will be noticed if we show up in your village.

"He's an energy eater, and a murderer. He's killed in

14

the past—at least fourteen victims—when he last escaped. We fear he'll up his body count, and we can't afford this to be a stumbling block in negotiations with the Witchblood Queen and our King. This could end our negotiations and send us back to the cold war days when Fae and witchblood were at odds. So do what you can, track him down, and destroy him. We need you to maintain the balance.

"You will report to me on Sunday noon with any progress you have made. Come to the fork in the trail and take the portal crossroads at midday.—Briar"

I stared at the letter. "Crap. I can't believe he wants me to take on this creature. I can't imagine how difficult this is going to be. I can't do it by myself, but he insists that I don't tell Rowan."

"Your grandmother would be obligated to tell the Court about it. I'm surprised you aren't expected to do the same."

"Technically, I suppose I should, since I belong to the Crystal Cauldron, but I can see how the Fae would blur lines on this. I don't even know what a sluagh is, let alone how to destroy one." I leaned back against the bench. "What should I do? If I don't obey, I'll be breaking my promise to him and that would be *very, very bad*, from what I understand."

"It would be, yes. I suggest you talk to your coworkers and enlist their help." Rebecca glanced warily at the trail. "Whatever you do, don't ignore this. You do *not* want the Overkings on your bad side. Briar isn't just some lower-echelon peasant in the Fae society. He has power, and he's smart. And if you cross him, he'll never stop hunting you."

I shivered. The day was still warm, but now it felt cold and lonely.

"All right, I'll contact him. Do you know what a sluagh is?"

Rebecca thought for a moment. "I know the name. I know they're dangerous. I'm not sure what they look like—they're sub-Fae so they won't look human, and they're also strong and capable of tearing apart a grown man."

That didn't sound good.

I grimaced. "All right. I'll meet him on Sunday." I paused, then said, "Can I talk to you about something that worries me?" I didn't expect that she'd have a heart to heart with me, but I couldn't find enough first-hand information with the Fae in all the studies I'd done. There *were* some people who worked with them, but most of them kept the Fae's secrets to themselves.

"What is it?" Rebecca looked curious.

I didn't exactly trust her, but I had enough interactions with her that I was certain she wouldn't lie to me. She might not answer, but she had nothing to gain by being dishonest.

"When I met him last summer, Briar was...mesmerizing. I need to know how to ward myself against that. If I can't talk to Rowan about this, then I'm not sure what to do." I blushed. What I wanted to say was that Briar seemed to have the ability to turn me on, and I didn't want anything to happen because of that. I trusted myself, but I didn't trust him.

Rebecca smiled slyly, disconcerting on the face of what seemed like a lovely young girl. But her eyes—they belied her impish nature. "I see. Yes, I know what you're talking about. Luckily, the Fae guiles don't work on demons like me. My advice is that you wear iron hidden on your body, and that you work on a mental shield that can block him from getting into your mind. Or you can just drink mugwort and pepper-mint tea, and that should help."

I nodded. The Fae hated iron, I knew that much. "Won't I antagonize him if I wear something with iron in it?"

"Probably, but it will keep him from touching you. But he

won't know if you drink the tea, and it will help guard against his magnetism. That will keep him from getting into your mind, and it's probably stronger than the iron itself." She stood. "I've delivered my message."

"What did he promise you in return for doing so? I'm curious." When we wanted to encourage or thank Rebecca for her help, Killian barbecued up a rack of ribs and she devoured them. But I wondered what the Fae could offer her.

Rebecca paused, then looked over her shoulder at me. "My life. I may not answer to him, but even I'm not stupid enough to refuse to play messenger. And so, I live another day." She vanished into the forest just as the clouds rolled over, blocking out the sun.

I glanced at the sky as I headed back to my house. We weren't due for rain, but the clouds were a perfect foil to my hope that the next few weeks—or months—would be free of stress and worry. Frowning, I shut the door behind me, and not even the cats zooming by, chasing each other, could make me smile.

CHAPTER THREE

ONE THING I MISSED FROM MY HOUSE WAS THE WRAP-around porch, so Killian had hired Jim Lark of Jim Lark 'n Sons to build one on our house. Jim had supervised renovations on my own house, and we knew and trusted him. His crew had started in mid-March and were finished by the end of April, and now we had a lovely wrap-around enclosed porch like the one I was used to. I could sit outside and drink coffee on mornings that were warm enough, and that was all I needed to be perfectly happy to make our new home in Killian's house.

I fixed a triple latte and, together with a tuna sandwich, I sat out on the porch, contemplating my life. Everything had changed so much in the past five years. My ex was now in prison for most of the rest of his life, for trying to kill both me and Killian. I had left the big city and moved back to Moonshadow Bay. I worked—except for this sabbatical—for a paranormal investigations company. I had seen things I never knew existed, and I had pushed myself into doing more than I ever thought I could. I had met the love of my life, and

I was now the wife of a wolf shifter. All in all, a complete 180, from a life of stifling frustration and neglect to a life filled with wonder and love. If I could just get my best friend back, I'd be absolutely thrilled.

I brought out my phone and, after a moment, texted Killian.

BRIAR SENT ME A MESSAGE VIA REBECCA. HE'S CALLING IN MY DEBT. THERE'S A CREATURE ROAMING THE TOWN THAT I HAVE TO FIND BEFORE IT BEGINS KILLING PEOPLE. THE FAE LET IT ESCAPE, AND THEY WANT IT BACK BUT CAN'T OPENLY GO HUNTING, SO BRIAR ASKED ME TO FIND AND DESTROY IT.

Sure enough, within a few seconds, Killian answered. CRAP. WHAT'S THE CREATURE CALLED? HOW DANGEROUS IS IT? CAN YOU ENLIST YOUR GRANDMOTHER FOR HELP?

NO, I answered. APPARENTLY THE FAE ARE IN NEGOTIA-TIONS WITH THE COURT MAGIKA AND THIS COULD DISRUPT MATTERS. SINCE ROWAN IS AN OFFICER OF THE COURT, I CAN'T TELL HER ABOUT IT. I THOUGHT I'D ASK TAD AND THE OTHERS AT CONJURE INK IF THEY CAN HELP ME.

GOOD IDEA. After a pause, Killian added: JUST BE CAUTIOUS. I KNOW YOU CAN'T IGNORE THE REQUEST, BUT YOU'RE GOING TO KEEP ME APPRISED ABOUT EVERYTHING THAT HAPPENS AND I'M GOING TO HELP YOU. NO QUESTIONS ABOUT IT, SO DON'T EVEN PROTEST.

I WON'T. Then, smiling, I added, I LOVE YOU MORE THAN YOU CAN IMAGINE.

AND I LOVE YOU MORE THAN YOU'LL EVER KNOW. I'VE GOT TO GET BACK TO WORK. HEAVY DAY TODAY AND I'LL BE LATE. DON'T WAIT DINNER ON ME.

As I texted back my love and signed off, the sun broke through again and the tangy, lazy smell of summer coming in swept over me. I was a lucky woman, and I was glad that I knew that.

TAD, CAITLIN, AND HANK WERE BOTH SURPRISED AND
happy to see me when I arrived at work. Wren was out again
—her husband Walter had had a bad fall and she was gone for
a couple of days until he could heal up. The experimental
medication that he was on wasn't working, and I wondered if
he'd been assigned a placebo. It was in a blind trial and Wren
and Walter wouldn't know until the treatment had run its
course. For the past few weeks, I'd had the uncomfortable
feeling that Walter wouldn't make it out of this alive. MS
could be so many things to so many people, but he was deteri-
orating quickly, and his body seemed determined to buck all
the meds.

"So, how's the life of leisure?" Tad asked. I knew he was
joking, so I just laughed at the crack. "What can we do for
you?"

I sighed. "You can welcome me back part time, at least?
I'm kind of done staying at home 24/7. I'm still working on
the book, but I need to get out of the house more often. I
brought a case with me," I added, dangling the bait.

Tad perked up. "You want to come back? I thought for
sure at least you'd be out the summer."

"Well, you lose that bet," I said. "Seriously, I am not cut
out to sit at home all day with my thoughts. When I was
running the magazine, I was at work everyday, even when I
was writing the articles to go in it."

"So, what's the case you're bringing in?" Caitlin said.

I glanced around the new *new* office. Tad and Caitlin now
lived in the house to which we'd originally moved Conjure
Ink, and now, the business was settled into a former dance
studio from decades past. It was a comfortable place, with a
few spirits who were welcome to stay because they were so
likable. It felt good to be back in a professional setting, and

with Tad no longer living on premises, we could dedicate all the space to Conjure Ink.

"Can we sit?" I motioned to the round table. It was the one thing that consistently moved with us. Or, rather, it was the one thing that spelled out Conjure Ink to me. We sat at it when brainstorming and for all staff meetings. It had unwittingly become the heart and soul of the company. A place where everyone was equal, and all our voices mattered.

As we gathered around the table, I felt the gentle touch of Miss Penny. Penelope Finch, the dance teacher who had long ago owned Miss Penny's Dance & Music Academy, had stuck around. She was well aware she was dead, but she wasn't quite ready to move on yet. Her spirit was a gentle one, though, and she liked people. She liked them so much, she had stayed in this plane, wanting to make contact on some level.

I smiled and glanced over my shoulder. I could barely see her there—or at least, the outline of her aura. "Thanks, Miss Penny. I'm glad to see you, too."

"Penny here?" Caitlin asked.

Hank nodded. "Yeah, I can see her. I have to say, I enjoy her company."

"When I was here alone at night a few weeks ago, I felt completely safe. It felt like she was keeping an eye on the door, and I never once felt uneasy. I like having her here," Caitlin said.

"I was thinking I want to get her story," I said. "I'd like to know why she's staying here. If there's something she feels she left unfinished, I might be able to help her." At their looks, I held up my hand. "I know, I know. We all like Miss Penny, but if she has unfinished business, it's only right to help her figure it out. If she's just hanging out because she wants to, that's another matter."

"All right, if you insist. Go ahead and mark that down on your to-do list. So, what's this case you have? We could use something to sink our teeth into. It's been too quiet lately. I'm wondering if things are just gearing up for a busy summer on the paranormal side of things." Tad pulled out his notebook.

"Okay, this is going back to our ill-fated camping trip. Remember Briar?"

Tad's face drained, as did Hank's. Caitlin let out a groan.

"That's right, he's calling in his favor. In the grand scheme of things, it's not horrible. In fact, I think I'm getting off easy, to be honest." I handed Briar's note to Tad. "Here, read this. Rebecca gave it to me this morning. He enlisted her to deliver it."

Tad read it, whistled, and then handed it to Caitlin. Hank leaned in, reading over her shoulder. After they finished, they handed it back to me. Tad was already tapping away on his laptop.

"Well, what do you think?" I asked.

"I'm looking up the sluagh right now. I assume you haven't had time to research," he said, squinting at the screen.

"Right. I was thinking we could search the databases here to see if there's any lore on them. Also, we can't consult Rowan. If the Court Magika finds out that the Fae have lost track of a dangerous member of the sub-Fae, then there's going to be trouble. And if I leak it, then Briar's going to be on my ass about it. I don't want to make the Overkings angry." I frowned. "It would help if I knew what the sluagh looks like."

Tad worried his lip, deep in his search. "I'm looking."

"I'm getting some coffee. January, want some?" Caitlin stood, heading toward the break room. Tad had outfitted it to fit my suggestions when we first looked at the place.

"Thanks, but I'm still finishing my latte." I held up my cup.

"I've never dealt with the Fae except on the periphery of

other issues," Hank said. "They're cunning and quick to twist words and meanings." He grimaced and I had the feeling he was still feeling guilty for being the cause of this whole situation. I not only needed their help, but this would go a long ways to finally settling all the disruption caused by our ill-fated attempt to hunt down Bigfoot on Hank's insistence.

"That they are," I said. "Maybe you can help me. I spoke to Rebecca because I remember how hypnotic Briar was. She suggested that I maybe wear something with iron in it—"

"No, that would be a big mistake. Yes, it would keep them away from you, but Briar would take it as a huge insult if you even came near him with iron."

"She also suggested peppermint and mugwort tea."

"That will help. We can stop him from getting his hooks in you, but wearing iron? Bad idea." He leaned back and folded his arms across his chest.

"I thought so," I said. "I told her I wasn't going to wear iron."

"Got it!" Tad turned his laptop around so we could see. "I found this in the database of one of the sites overseen by Urban Legends." Urban Legends was an umbrella group for several organizations like Conjure Ink. Tad had pulled it together so we could all combine our info and build an amazing library of events and creatures.

The screen showed several terrifying pictures. The creature in question was short and squat, with spindly legs that looked too thin to hold up the barrel-shaped torso. The arms were long and spindly as well, and the body reminded me of Fungus out of *Monsters, Inc.* The sluagh's mottled, tan torso was partly squishy, partly fuzzy, and the creature had one central eye, like a cyclops. Inside of its gash of a mouth, sharp, needle-like teeth glistened.

"How tall is it?" Caitlin asked, before I had the chance.

"It says here that this one was about five feet tall. I've

found several accounts mentioning their height range as between four to five feet or so. They are rarely seen, and the last known encounter—when these pictures were taken—was from 1974. Apparently, the Fae have gotten better at keeping them away from human society." Tad enlarged the article, which was taken from a microfiche copy of a magazine. "This account comes from June 8, 1974. It was printed in a journal called *Everyday Myths & Monsters* that went out of business in 1992."

Janet and Tyler Mason never expected to be attacked by a sluagh—one of the Celtic sub-Fae—when they were driving home to their farm in Terameth Lake. At eleven P.M., as they passed by Hell's Thicket, their car broke down. The couple got out to walk to the nearest gas station, but they had walked for no more than about five minutes when a creature broke through the bushes and made straight for them.

The creature was approximately five feet tall, and the body spread out from the spindly legs into a barrel-shaped torso, with long branch-like arms, a central eye that was as big as a human child's head, and tufts of hair between the legs. It was impossible to tell if there were genitals, so the sex of the creature was unknown.

However, the gaping mouth below the eye was wide and thin, with several rows of needle-shaped teeth. Before they could take another step, the creature gave chase and took down Tyler. It bit through his jugular before he could fight it off. Janet managed to climb a nearby tree, and the creature seemed unable to follow her, so it shambled off into the forest after eating part of Tyler's side and chest.

A police officer responded to reports of screams and

they found her in the tree. She managed to describe the creature to them before sliding into unconsciousness. When she regained consciousness, she was mute, and eventually, though doctors did their best to work with her, she slid into a state of catatonia. She was committed to a long-term care facility, where she eventually died. She never regained her awareness, and the only evidence police had, with regards to Tyler's death, was the account she had been able to give them and the pictures on her camera that she had taken before the creature attacked Tyler.

The autopsy exonerated her from any part in his death, and while some people thought a cougar had attacked them, the coroner said no large animal he knew of could cause that kind of damage and leave bite marks in the shape that they found on Tyler's torso. The case remains open to this day.

"How do they know it was a sluagh?" Caitlin asked.

Tad scanned the rest of the article. "Apparently, this group of paranormal investigators went in, thinking it was some sort of demon. They were actually ghost hunters, but they quickly discovered that the creature hadn't left—it was still there. They encountered it on the second day of their investigation, and it damned near killed the entire team. They got away, but every one of them was injured, and it turns out one of the Overkings—the Fae—saved them. The Fae managed to subdue the sluagh, and he warned the team to get the hell out of there. He let slip what they were fighting."

"And they got a picture of it," I said.

"Right. The other cases—the few there are—have similar stories," Tad said, leaning back in his chair.

"Well," I said. "Are you with me? Are we going to go sluagh hunting?"

Hank laughed. "You know we're in, January. Now, time to figure out how to find it, where to find it, and what to do with it."

Just like that, I was back at work.

CHAPTER FOUR

WE SPENT THE AFTERNOON READING OVER EVERY reference we could find to the sluagh. I thought of trying to contact Briar for more information, but that would only indebt me further. Maybe I could cadge more out of him when we met on Sunday, if I was careful.

"I'm trying to figure out where it could be. Maybe I should check with Millie to see if there have been any unexplained attacks in the past week?" Millie Tuptin was our local chief of police. A German shepherd shifter, she was good at her job, and we'd had altogether too many discussions over dangerous cases.

"That might be a good idea," Tad said.

I pulled out my phone and called her. Wonder of wonders, she was at her desk. "Hey, Millie, I have a question for you, and it's not just rhetorical. Has anyone reported any unexplained attacks or scary encounters as of the past week or so?"

"Hey, January. Nice to hear from you, and yes, actually, now that you mention it, we've had two reports of townsfolk being attacked by something they didn't recognize. Two men were hiking in Devil's Gulch and encountered a monster they couldn't identify. Well, the one left alive couldn't identify it. Whatever it was, it wasn't human—or humanoid—and it blends into the shadows and just seems to vanish." She paused, then asked, "Why did you ask? Do you know what this thing is?"

"Maybe," I said. "Can you come over to the office now? I'm back at work, at least part time, and I think this is a case we should discuss in person."

"I don't like the sound of that," she said. "I'll be over in fifteen minutes."

As she hung up, I turned to the others. "She'll be here in fifteen. She said there have been cases of unexplained attacks in the past week by something that isn't humanoid. I'm thinking it's the sluagh. According to the references, the creature feeds on human flesh."

"I'm almost hoping that the encounters are related. That would give us a direction in which to look," Tad said.

"Me too." Hank rose to pour himself another cup of coffee. "Anybody else?"

Caitlin raised her mug. "I'll go for another."

I took the opportunity to call Killian. He was on his lunch break. "Hey sweetie, I just wanted to let you know that I'm at the office."

"You're at work?" He sounded surprised, but not concerned.

"Yeah, I've decided I need to start back to work again. I'll begin with part time and see how my ERS handles it. I think I should be fine. I've got a lot to tell you tonight, so I'll bring home pizza for dinner and it will keep till you get home."

"Don't bother saving dinner for me," he said. "We're going to order in here since it's going to be a long evening."

"No worries. I can always eat the leftovers for lunch tomorrow." I blew kissing noises through the phone, then hung up. "While we're waiting for Millie, what's the news? I feel like I've missed out on a lot."

Tad and Caitlin glanced at each other. "Shall we tell them?" he asked.

Caitlin nodded. "Since January's here, yes."

"Tell us what?" Hank asked.

"I hoped Wren would be here too, but given how her schedule is so erratic lately, I'll just call her," Caitlin said.

Tad slid his arm around Caitlin. "We're getting married!"

I jumped up and clapped, hugging first Caitlin, then Tad.

"Woohoo! I figured once you two actually got together that it would go fast." Over the past couple years I'd watched the pair orbit around each other, never quite meeting. I had also known—thanks to their confidences—that they were both interested in each other, but they'd been afraid of spoiling their friendship. Finally, I meddled a little, they took the plunge, and now—they were getting married.

"I knew you two were right for each other," Hank said. "I'm so pleased!"

"Pleased enough to be my best man?" Tad asked.

Hank blushed and ducked his head. "You want that, given the..." He motioned to Tad's cane. Tad had recently discovered that his recovery had progressed about as far as it was going to. He'd needed liver surgery after Bigfoot just about killed him, and now he was stuck walking with a cane forever. He'd sustained a lot of damage other than his liver, as well.

"Of course. You're my bro, you know?"

Caitlin turned to me. "And would you be my matron of honor, January?"

I blinked, tearing up. Caitlin had been ousted from her Pride when she broke away from an arranged marriage. She literally had no family left who claimed her. "Of course I will. I'd be happy to stand by you."

At that moment, the door opened and Millie entered the

office. She glanced over at Wren's desk. "Walter having another bad day?" she asked. Her voice was soft. Everybody who knew Wren adored the woman, and we all watched, feeling helpless, doing what we could, when we could. But it never felt like enough.

"Yeah," Tad said, frowning. "It's getting more frequent. I hate to say it, but I don't think..."

"He doesn't," I said. "I've been reticent on the subject, and of course I'd never mention it to Wren, though I'm sure she knows, but Walter's on the fast track out of this realm. The past few times I talked to her, I could feel his energy back there, and he's waning. It breaks my heart."

"A sobering note, but I think you're right," Hank said. "I can feel it too."

"Well, we're not here to speculate on Walt's health," Caitlin said. "I mean, I think so too, but let's focus on what we *can* do something about."

"What have you got for me?" Millie asked. "I brought pictures of the victims. One's going to live, but he's pretty sliced up. The other's dead. Whatever the creature is, it took a bite out of both of them. Nasty wounds, and the victim who survived has a raging infection. The doctor has it under control but it's required IV antibiotics to do so. Not as bad as a Komodo dragon's bite, but far worse than any dog or cat bite."

She tossed a couple file folders on the table. "I would have just emailed these, but we haven't had a chance to scan the pictures in and the paperwork is still waiting on our data entry clerks." As she headed over to pour herself a cup of coffee, Tad pulled the files over in front of him.

I sat on one side of him, and Millie sat on the other. Caitlin and Hank settled down as close as they could. Tad flipped open the file and sorted out the pictures. Millie was right. The bite was nasty—as were the slashes across their arms and legs. Both victims were men, and neither looked weak.

"You said this happened in Devil's Gulch?"

Devil's Gulch was a ravine on the distant outskirts of town. It was seldom used or visited, and it was overgrown with vegetation. I wasn't familiar with why people avoided it, but my instincts had always kept me from even getting near it.

"Yes. Here, these pics show the bites." Millie paused, then said, "What have you got for me? Do you know what we're dealing with? You must have had some reason to ask about attacks today."

"We do, actually," I said. "You remember when I told you about my little bargain with the Fae—how I owe them a favor?"

She nodded. "Yeah... Oh, I assume they've called it in?"

"Right. This needs to remain private—I can't have the news getting around, but it might give you a leg up on the investigation. Maybe we can work together."

Millie frowned. "What do you mean, 'private'? How can we work on a case if we can't talk about it?"

"Millie, we have to. The information can't get out." I held Millie's gaze. "I'm serious about this—if word gets out, my life could be in danger. I wouldn't put it past them."

"Past who? Is somebody blackmailing you?"

"The Fae are negotiating with the Court Magika right now. They can't have anything of this nature slip out." That was all I had to say.

Millie stiffened. "Okay, I see. All right, I'll keep this as private as I can. No need to say more."

I nodded. "This could affect those delicate negotiations. Briar specifically told me I'm not to let them get wind of what's happened."

Millie thought for a moment. "And you're okay with keeping this quiet from your grandmother?"

I nodded. "I have to be. I honestly don't think it would shake things up as much as Briar seems to think, but I'm not willing to fuck around and find out. I owe him a favor, a favor that saved Tad and Hank. I owe him two lives' worth of reciprocation."

"All right, tell me what's going on," she said after a moment's contemplation.

"What's going on is that they accidentally let a sluagh get loose. The creature's in town, prowling around, and they want me to destroy it. Not return it, but destroy it." I told her what we had learned about the creature.

"Then you truly do need to take it out. And I understand why Briar didn't want you to say anything. To be honest, I know a little about the negotiations going on. I wasn't going to say anything, because this is dicey, explosive territory. But at this point, you're correct. It wouldn't be wise to tell your grandmother or any power player in the Court Magika about this situation. The Fae are attempting to connect to the world around them, after all these thousands of years of self-exile, and something like this could muddy the waters."

"Is *that* what the negotiations are about?" The thought of the Fae mingling with townsfolk seemed absurd.

Millie nodded. "The Fae are looking to join society, like the vampires did decades ago. But as I said, it's a delicate balance. They're more arrogant than the vamps were, and more volatile. However, if they don't manage to find their place in the modern world, they won't be able to keep their sacred grounds without resorting to a war on the world around them. And they would not win—and they know it."

"So they're desperate, and their egos have been stung? That's not a good combo," Tad said.

"No, it isn't. And something as simple as this sluagh could

truly topple the delicate dance of diplomacy going on at this moment," Millie said. "I've probably told you more than is wise, but if you're involved in this matter—and I understand that you have no choice—then you really should understand the stakes."

I let out a long breath. "I kind of wish I didn't know. But you're right. We're playing a political game of Jenga right now."

"Good analogy," Millie said. "Anyway, this creature sounds like the same one who attacked my victims. The survivor couldn't give a good description except that it made him think of a cyclops, only smaller than those in legend." Millie sorted through the reports in the files.

"That sounds about right," I said. "The sluagh like to eat people."

She grimaced. "Delightful. All right, call me for whatever assistance you need." She glanced at me. "I should temporarily deputize one of you, so I can assign officers to help you if need be."

I shook my head. "Nope, don't pick me, please. If I get a sudden migraine and have to duck out, you want somebody here who can still run the show."

"Hank," Tad said. "Deputize Hank."

Hank rolled his eyes. He liked being classified and labeled as much as he liked tech that was twenty years out of date. But he just cleared his throat and nodded. "I'll do it."

"All right. That will give my men someone to answer to. I'll put Tyson and Cece on call. They're both good at keeping their mouths shut, and they're seasoned. Cece can take the lead. She's led a number of investigations. I'll tell them it's on an NDA unless I give the go-ahead." She stared at the pictures we had dug up. "That's one nasty-looking beast."

"I'm not even sure what its vulnerabilities are. I'm supposed to meet Briar on Sunday. If we haven't caught this thing by then—I'll press him for more information, as long as it doesn't create another deal. With the ERS, this, and the Crow Man, I feel like my life isn't my own anymore. At least the shadow man's off my back now."

"That was hard enough," Tad said. "All right, let's get back to work. See if you can find any references to what it might be vulnerable to—fire, maybe? Water? Anything that might give us a leg up on the critter."

With that, Millie said her goodbyes and left. I slid right back into work mode and, after changing my password on my work computer—we changed them every few months and Tad had a database of new and old passwords—I brought up a screen and dove into what I could find out about the sluagh. But in the back of my mind, I was thinking about what was at stake, and why we had to keep this quiet. I hated keeping things from my grandmother, but this time, it was necessary. The question was: could we discover this creature, take it down, and fulfill my favor to Briar without her finding out?

CHAPTER FIVE

"Here it is!" I jumped up, pointing to my screen. I'd been searching for about two hours and had finally found a reference to someone in 1871 who had managed to kill one of the sluagh.

The sluagh attacked a farmer who happened to have an iron pitchfork with him. He managed to stab it, and not only did he pierce it in the center, between the eye and the legs, but the iron sizzled as it touched the sluagh and burned it so badly, he was able to kill it. The farmer hurried to the doctor, then, after getting his wounds tended, he took a group of friends out there to collect the body, and to figure out what it was, but by then the creature turned into a mass of goo and soaked into the ground. While they found sludge where it had fallen, there was nothing to prove the farmer had actually fought what he said he did.

"So iron will burn it, which is typically anathema against the Fae. And it can be damaged with a regular weapon, since the pitchfork apparently wounded it." Tad jotted down a few notes. "You said that Briar wants this creature dead?"

I nodded. "As a doornail. He specifically instructed me to destroy it. In other words, I'm charged with getting rid of the evidence." I frowned. "As to finding out where it is, we at least have some place to start, given the attacks happened in Devil's Gulch."

Hank nodded. "I can help there," he said. "I've got a number of friends who hang out on the...shadow side...of the world. There are two of them here in town. They keep track of things that might escape the police's notice. Some beefs and disagreements run below the surface and are better kept out of the light. They might know if something's hanging out in the Gulch."

"Speaking of shadows, I wonder if Val Slater might know anything about this. He's almost always got his finger on the pulse of the town."

It had been a while since I'd talked to Val. He had stuck to his promise to leave Killian and me alone. The godfather of vampires, at least in this area, Val had developed an oddball crush on me early on when I returned to Moonshadow Bay, and he had taken delight in needling Killian.

After I confronted him, he backed off, and I had to say, he'd been good to his word about it. But Val had another side. He quietly and unobtrusively shored up several charities, and he had sunk a lot of money into helping the disadvantaged in town. Val was also known for having his finger on the pulse of what Hank had called the "underground" and if anybody knew the whereabouts of the sluagh, it would likely be Val.

I put in a call to Val's assistant. Daniel Ashante spoke for Val during the day, as well as acting as his personal secretary.

I'd never call him a friend, but he was definitely an acquaintance, given the years we'd known each other.

"Daniel, this is January Jaxson. I need to talk to Val about something. Can you have him call me tonight? I'll be home all evening."

"Will do. Val will be glad to hear from you," he added. "Is your number the same?"

"Yeah, it is." I thanked him and hung up. "Well, I think I'm going to go home and rest a bit. I don't have a migraine, but I don't want to aggravate the ERS by working too hard at first. But it sure feels good to be back," I added.

"It's good to have you back," Tad said. "We've missed you. You belong *here*, January, even if you are writing a book."

I nodded. "I think working with all of you is going to help make that book actually happen. I'm not that good at being my own boss," I added, grinning. "Not everybody's cut out for the nine-to-five, but it helps me focus. Okay, I'll see you Monday!" And with that, I transferred the research I'd done to my tablet so I could think about it at home, gathered my things, and headed for the door.

I STOPPED BY THE NEAREST PAPA MONROE'S PIZZA-TO-GO and picked up a couple pies, one Hawaiian, and one sausage, pepperoni, extra cheese, and pineapple. Both Killian and I liked fruit on our pizzas, though pineapple was our only real choice. After filling up my car with gas and stopping by the grocery store for whole bean coffee and berries for dessert, I eased into the driveway and set the pizza on the landing at the top of the side stairs. A quick dash to the mailbox to collect the mail, and I was ready to go in.

I glanced over at my old house. I missed it in some ways. I'd grown up there with my parents. Ari and I had sequestered ourselves in my bedroom, talking about boys and school and our plans for the future. Those walls held so many memories, though not all of them pleasant. But now, the memories weren't all mine. With my in-laws living there, they would create new ones with my sister-in-law's children. And the ears of the house would listen and remember.

I picked up the pizzas and was trying to balance both them and the mail while fishing out my key.

"Can I help?"

I turned around. Serena stood there, a wide smile on her face. She and William had welcomed me in like one of their own. I had to admit, shifters—especially the wolves—adopted people into their families, and there was never any doubt of whether you belonged. If they loved you, you knew.

"Yes, please," I said, handing her the pizzas. I found my keys and unlocked the door, ushering her inside before I followed. She carried the pizzas to the table and set them there.

"I saw you out the window," she said. "You looked like you could use a hand."

"You were certainly right about that." I tossed the mail on the table and set my purse beside it. "Want some coffee? And by coffee, I mean a latte or mocha?"

"I'd love an iced caramel latte." Serena sat down. She was well-acquainted with my passion for caffeine, and she seemed to find it amusing. "A double shot. I've got to help William tonight with the bills and accounts." Serena settled at the table while I flipped on the espresso machine.

A tall woman, Serena was sturdy and athletic. Both Killian and Tally reflected their parents' looks, from the wheaten hair to the green eyes to the long, smooth noses.

"Do you miss teaching?" I asked.

"Some days, yes. I've actually decided to open a preschool run on the lines of the Jullian School." The Jullian methodology of teaching was to shifters what Montessori was to humans. "I've applied to the city for permits. I found a space that would be perfect for it—there's an empty convenience store on Laguna Way. I can't run it at home since William needs to focus on his work."

Instead of renting a commercial space, William had taken over what had been the hidden ritual room and turned it into his home office. Since I had renovated it to be an actual basement instead of having a trapdoor for an entrance, the lower floor was now a nice space, and all the ghosts and chaotic energies were long gone.

"Really? You'd be great at running a Jullian school. Do they charge a lot for a franchise?"

She shook her head. "It doesn't work like that in the shifter world. Once we're trained, anybody can open up one as long as they have that certificate hanging on the wall. But the city requires permits, so I'm at that stage right now. And that way, I can take care of Victoria and Leanna whenever Tally needs me to, and she can go back to work. I know she misses working outside the house."

I handed her the iced latte and pulled another for myself. I sat down opposite her at the table and pointed to the pizzas. "I'm going to pop these in the oven now. You want to eat dinner with me? Killian's holding his monthly spay and neuter clinic today, so he won't be home until late."

Serena eyed the pizzas, her eyes bright. That was one thing about shifters—they had hearty appetites and I never felt like I had to stick to salads around them.

"Well, William *is* planning on having the guys over to watch a baseball game. They're going to eat us out of house and home. I told him the men can make their own sandwiches. I was just planning on reading in my office, so sure—I'll stay for pizza."

I preheated the oven and slid the pizzas onto baking

sheets, then tucked them in to bake. While we waited, we chatted about life in general. I seldom mentioned the nature of my work, because even though she tried to restrain her nervousness, I knew that my occupation made Serena uneasy. Most wolf shifters had serious issues with magic. It wasn't that they didn't approve, but it just made most of them jittery. There was something about the energy that didn't settle well in their aura. And that included phenomena like ghosts, demons, and anything else that you could think of in that realm. So I did my best to make Killian's parents comfortable. I was lucky that Killian had grown beyond that nervousness.

But I did tell her that I went back to work. "I love writing, but I love people too, so I decided that I'll just take longer to write the book, and then go back to work part time. Tad's glad I'm coming back."

"Will it disrupt your headaches?" Serena and William weren't quite sure what to think about my energy reflux syndrome, but they never once indicated they didn't believe it was real, like some people did about invisible disabilities. I never once felt gaslighted or like they thought I was faking it.

"I hope not. We'll see. I'm doing better, now that I'm practicing a lot more magic, but it will never be the same as if my mother had brought me up to actually use my powers." I paused, thinking about the whole situation. "But I don't blame her. Not now that I understand why she did it—and there were several reasons."

We ate and went on to chat about the shared garden we were working on for the two households. Killian and William had built a large patch of raised beds and we were growing a large kitchen garden together. The men had also planted several apple trees for us and a couple pear trees.

Finally, Serena glanced at her watch. It was seven-thirty. "I'd better go. Thank you for dinner and coffee. See you later, dear." She kissed me on the cheek and squeezed my hand before heading out the kitchen door. I cleared the plates and our latte tumblers, then rinsed them and tucked them into the dishwasher. After wrapping up the leftover pizza, I wandered into the living room and decided to write for a while.

A little over an hour later, the phone rang.

I glanced at the caller ID. "Hey Val, how are you?"

Val's voice, smooth as butter, poured out. "Everything's good," he said. "So, what can I do for you, January?"

"Sorry about interrupting you, Val. I need to ask you something. Have you heard any odd reports about strange creatures hanging around, especially near Devil's Gulch?" I described the sluagh to him. "I don't think they can form-shift," I added.

He was silent for a moment, then slowly said, "There's a sluagh running around?"

Bingo. He knew what they were.

"Yeah, but I can't talk about it more than to tell you that I've been charged with finding and destroying it. But in order to get rid of it, I first have to *find* the creature." I licked my lips.

"Oh good gods, you're working for the *Fae* now? What are you, their hitwoman?"

I could practically see him rolling his eyes.

"Well…in this case, yes. I am. And I'll be in big trouble if I don't deliver on this. So, help a woman out and just tell me what you know, if anything?" I didn't like using my "cajoling" voice as I called it—it felt a little sleazy—but Val responded to it, and I needed whatever info I could gather.

He was silent for a moment. Then, he said, "Of course I'll help you if I can. You know you can always ask me for favors."

I stretched out on the sofa, sitting against the arm of the sofa and stared at my feet. "Thank you. I doubt if I can reciprocate, but if I can, you know you can call me." I knew better than promise anything to a vampire. I just wished I hadn't had to promise anything to Briar.

"I don't expect anything in return," Val said. "You chose the wolf. You're happily married—at least I hope you are. We're...solid acquaintances."

That stung, though he was right. "Acquaintances, not friends?"

Val's voice shifted, becoming more professional—meaning, aloof. "As the Dowager Countess of Grantham said, 'We are allies, my dear, which can be a good deal more effective.' So, not *friends*. But we have mutual respect, and that is something money cannot buy, because it requires a certain amount of loyalty."

I exhaled slowly. He was right on that—money didn't promise loyalty. If you could be bought by one person, then someone with a higher price could also buy your secrets. And he was also right in that we weren't friends. My ego was just a little bruised, but it shouldn't be.

"You're right. And sometimes yes, allies are better than friends. Can you check around, and the sooner the better?"

"Of course. I'll call you tomorrow night—"

"Thanks, Val. I hope you're doing well," I said.

"I truly believe you mean that. I'm good. No worries. I'll talk to you tomorrow night," he added, and then, with a brief goodbye, he hung up.

As the line went dead, it hit me how tired I was. Most of the weariness was emotional, but I decided I'd go to bed early with a movie and the cats. Killian would probably be home before I fell asleep.

I had no sooner snuggled in bed when the phone rang again. This time, it was Ari.

"Hi," I said, trying to keep my voice aloof. I didn't want to seem overeager. "What's up?"

"Hey," she said, sounding embarrassed. "I thought I'd call because..."

I waited for a moment, then decided to save the phone call. "I'm glad you called. How are the kids? How are you?" I missed her children. I didn't ever want any of my own, but I liked playing auntie to LaKirk and Emily, as much as I enjoyed being auntie for Victoria and Leanna.

Ari cleared her throat, but her voice was stilly raspy. "Look, can we meet? I want... I need to talk about us. I've been stupid."

I tried to restrain myself, but my heart leapt as I made plans to meet her at my house for coffee, at ten. I knew Meagan had instigated this—it was our plan—but I acted surprised. "I'm looking forward to seeing you," I said. "Tomorrow, then."

After hanging up, I changed into a nightgown and crawled into bed with the remote. Things were moving—maybe slower than I liked—but I seemed to always find the help I needed. Grateful, I leaned back and turned on the television. I was ready for some mindless entertainment. With Xi and Klaus at my side, I snuggled under the covers, and before Killian could make it home, I slid off into dreamland.

CHAPTER SIX

THE NEXT MORNING, I WAS FIGHTING BUTTERFLIES IN MY stomach. While Ari and I had talked on the phone briefly a few times, this would be the first time we'd seen each other in person since our big fight a few months ago.

Since tonight was game night and I'd promised lasagna, I calmed myself by sauteing onions and garlic in a skillet, then added ground beef and spices. After it was ready, I spooned the mixture into a slow cooker. Adding tomato sauce, I turned it on low to simmer through the day.

I never trusted using the recipes where the noodles supposedly cooked while the lasagna was baking, so I boiled the noodles to an al dente state, rinsed them under cool water, then put them away. Finally, I grated the mozzarella and parmesan, and whipped the ricotta with herbs.

"There, everything is ready. All I have to do is build the lasagna and bake." I glanced at the time, then set out a plate of cookies on the kitchen table, debating whether I should make coffee now, or offer Ari a latte when she arrived.

"You'd think I was going on my first date or something," I muttered to myself.

A moment later, the doorbell rang. As I answered, I steeled myself. Meagan had promised that she'd get Ari to come around, but I wasn't sure how she intended to do that and I wasn't sure she had managed it.

I opened the door. Ari stood there with her short coppery pixie cut, weighing all of a hundred and five pounds. She was barely more than five feet, but she was a dynamo in a small package. And as I stared at her, I realized just how much I missed her.

"Ari…" I wasn't sure what to say, so I stood back, inviting her in. She followed me into the kitchen and sat down, looking around. Not much had changed in a few months, but it felt like it had been years since we'd spoken. At least, to me.

"Hey," she said. After another moment, Ari sighed and leaned back in her chair. "Meagan and I had a long talk. I… I'm sorry. She didn't feel at all like I thought she would."

I wondered whether to reveal that Meagan had showed up on my doorstep. If I *didn't* tell Ari, how would she feel if she found out later? Duped? Foolish? I wasn't sure, but I didn't want to find out the hard way.

"Meagan visited me yesterday. I thought she was going to tell me to stay away from the two of you—the four of you, now. But she didn't." I ducked my head. "I'm only telling you this because I don't want any misunderstandings, you know?"

Ari processed this, then nodded. "Yeah, to be honest, she told me she was going to talk to you. In fact… I asked her to. I was too embarrassed to broach the subject. I crossed the line, and she made me see that. Yes, it can be dangerous to be around you, given what you do. But just living in Moon-shadow Bay is dangerous, and there's always going to be something out there just waiting to get you. She made me see that we'll always face the chance of someone trying to snatch the kids, or spirits wreaking havoc on our lives, or serial killers hiding in the dark. So...I want to apologize. I understand if you need time to think about this—"

"No!" I jumped up, cutting her off. "I mean...I've missed you so much. You're my best friend. I'm not going to lie. Hearing you accuse me of being a danger to your kids hurt like hell. But I can see how you might be afraid. After all, a spirit possessed you, and it tried to force you to act in ways you would never choose to on your own. I'm sorry. I never meant for that to happen." I sank down in the seat next to her, tears welling in my eyes.

Ari held out her hands and I took them, giving them a squeeze.

"Nothing will ever separate us again. If I think you're on a case that's too dangerous, I'll just back out for a little bit till you're done. I'll keep the kids away if you're in the middle of something big." She exhaled a long, slow breath. "Do you forgive me?"

"Of course," I said, more because it felt like she needed to hear it rather than because I was holding a grudge. "I don't want to fight anymore. You're my sister, you know? Sisters of the heart. To be honest, I still feel horrible for backing away while I was with Ellison. I'd do it all differently if I had it to do over again."

She smirked. "He had control. Ellison hated anybody who was going to interfere with that abusive nature. So tell me, what are you working on now? Meagan said you quit to write a book? Let's catch up."

"I didn't quit. I took a sabbatical, but I'm going back part time starting next week. And yes, I'm trying to write a book, but I'm not enough of an introvert to write full time." I approached the coffee station. "What do you want?"

"Latte, three shots, vanilla caramel if you have it." She hesitated. "I heard through the grapevine that you sold your house?"

I began pulling shots for our lattes. "Right. To Killian's parents. It's nice having them next door. I know they'll take good care of my childhood home, and we can see Killian's parents anytime we want. Serena takes care of Tally's kids anytime there's a need."

Ari stared soberly at the cookies. "I wish I hadn't been so abrupt. It was the perfect place for a salon. I guess I need to look elsewhere."

"That might not be a bad thing," I said. "Money and friendship don't always mix. I don't want to play landlord, to be honest. This way, the house is off my hands and whatever they do with it is their choice." I brought our mugs over and handed her one. "Vanilla caramel, as you asked." As I sat down, I was practically vibrating, I was so happy.

"You might be right. Anyway, I did find another building for my salon that used to be one, so it has some equipment that comes with it, and I don't have to do any major renovations. I'm just going to paint, move a few things around, and add a seating area for clients." She worried her lip. "How do you like living next door to your in-laws?"

"Actually, I love it. Serena and William are lovely people, and they accept me in a way that I almost forgot. Rowan loves me, of course, and Teran, but Serena and William treat me like...well...it's almost like having my mother and father around. They're both nurturing people, and it feels like we have somebody watching out for us, you know?"

Ari nodded. "My folks live in Terameth Lake, along with my half-brother. Mom and Dad finally met Colton, and they're sorting out the relationship details. I think we're evolving, as a family. My sister's coming up from California in July and we're all going out camping together. A reunion of sorts, to seal the new aspects that have come out of find out about Colton."

"Are you looking forward to that?" I asked.

"Yes. No. Both. It's a lot, you know, and to add Emily and LaKirk joining our family at the same time, well... I have no clue how things will play out, but it's going to be interesting, that's for sure." She sipped her latte. "Meagan likes you. She also likes Killian. She told me I was being ridiculous back when I got angry. I didn't want to listen to her. But over the past few months, I've come to realize just how much I need you in my life—along with all the work you do."

"Well, buckle up, because I've got something new to face. Actually, something old, but it's going to resolve one of the stressors that's been hanging over my head for a while." I told her what was going on with Briar.

"Oh my gosh, you're going after a sluagh? I've done enough research to know how dangerous they are." She paled for a moment, then shook her head. "Promise me you'll be careful, January? I'm not afraid for myself, that's not why I'm asking you to be cautious. But they're dangerous creatures, the sub-Fae, and they have absolutely no conscience about killing anyone that gets in their path."

I cupped my hands around my mug. "I'll do whatever I can. I just know if I don't destroy this creature, Briar will be on my back. And having one of the Overkings angry at me is a worse fate than facing one of the sub-Fae." I hesitated, then said, "I called Val Slater last night to see if he could help. He said he'd call back tonight. I think he's over me, Ari. He called us acquaintances, not friends."

She studied my face for a moment. "That's a good thing, right?"

"Yeah, that's what I hoped would happen, actually. I want to keep a working relationship with him, but I needed him to respect my boundaries and Killian's boundaries. And it seems like he's doing just that." After that, we slid into catching up on the past few months' gossip, and by the time Ari had to leave to pick up the kids from their morning daycare—they'd let the nanny go down to afternoons only—we were back to where we'd been before.

Well, almost. There were still cracks in the fence, but we'd mended a lot of them, and we were ready to move back into our roles as best buds and cheerleaders, and that's exactly what I had hoped would happen.

AT ONE-THIRTY, I GOT A CALL FROM MILLIE. "WE HAVE another problem and it may be your sluagh," she said. "Can you come down to the station? I can't get away and I don't want to talk about this over the line."

I told her I'd be there in half an hour. After rinsing out our mugs, I made sure that the cats were set and I had a mixture of mugwort and peppermint tea, then headed down to the police station.

Downtown Moonshadow Bay was a lovely space, with a central building called City Central that covered an entire city block. Built of red brick, City Central encapsulated most of the town's government offices, including the police station, fire department, the Garrison Library, the PUD, the courthouse, and many other smaller spaces, including several restaurants.

The walls were painted in a warm lilac gray, and the floors were laminate, with a soundproof system that quieted the sounds of footsteps. There was a coziness to the complex, even as large as it was, and even though the jail was located in the police department, the energy was still smooth and muted.

I entered the bulletproof glass doors to the police station. The dispatcher waved at me. She recognized me from enough visits. I waved back and she buzzed me through, handing me a visitor's pass on a lanyard. I hung it around my neck, then made my way through the labyrinth of desks and cubicles. Some were manned with officers and clerks, while others were empty. By the time I reached the door leading to Millie's area, I had said hello to half a dozen familiar faces.

The officer nearest the door checked with dispatch before buzzing me through into the gleaming, cool hallway that led to Millie's office. I passed the restrooms, then stopped at an open door, peeking in to see Millie sitting there.

"Knock, knock," I said, poking my head around the open door.

"Come in!" She waved me in. "Have a seat. So, how are you?"

"Well, Ari and I made up. We're good again." Our argument had gotten around. In a small town like Moonshadow Bay, there wasn't much to do for some of the locals except gossip. Anything that was remotely interesting made the rounds like clockwork.

"Oh, thank heavens. You two were made for causing havoc together, and heaven help us if that got disrupted." But even in her snark, I could hear the genuine relief. She was friends with both of us, and it couldn't be easy when two of her friends were on the outs.

"So, what do you have for me?" I asked.

Millie handed me a file folder. "Warning, graphic imagery involved."

I steeled myself and opened the folder. "What am I looking at?" But then, I saw the words AUTOPSY REPORT across the top of one of the papers. "Oh...unexplained homicide?"

Millie nodded. "I think it's your creature. We found the victim—Dwayne Stephens—in a field next to Devil's Gulch this morning. He was roughed up pretty bad, and the marks are similar in nature to those of a big cat or a bear mauling, just like the first death. But the doctor confirms he's never seen anything quite like either case."

I took a deep breath and exhaled slowly, then began flipping through the report. I knew there were pictures at the end, and I was dreading them, but anything I could learn to help me understand the sluagh, the better. As I read about some of the damage done to the victim, I grimaced. But there was nothing to prepare me for the pictures.

The man had been eaten alive. Well, not all of him, but enough to know just how much pain he would have been in. Bite marks littered his body, deep gashes obviously made by teeth. Chunks of flesh had been ripped out. The worst was that his nose had been bitten off. I quickly closed the folder and slid it back across the desk.

"You said it happened next to Devil's Gulch?" I tried to focus on the peripheries of the murder, rather than the gory details.

She nodded. "I have to tell you, there's an energy to the gulch that scares the fuck out of just about everybody. Two of my officers found his body right beside the gulch this morning. A neighbor about two streets over usually jogs every morning along the street that runs parallel to the gulch. He saw the body from the road—the victim was wearing a bright yellow tank top. A.D. Anniston, our runner, wasn't sure what it was at first, so he darted into the turnout to find out, and saw the blood. A.D. immediately called the cops and then waited on the side of the road rather than next to the ravine. That was probably a good idea."

I nodded. She was correct. If the sluagh was hiding in the ravine, anybody close was fair game. "He's smart, at least. All right. And the medical examiner said it's not an animal attack?"

"She's never seen anything quite like it," Millie said. "You saw the pictures. It was worse in person, trust me. No animal did that. Not even a grizzly would leave such a mess. And there was no sign of a human's hand in it, either."

"All right. From everything I've heard so far, we have a place to start looking. I guess I'd better get home and come up with a game plan. I'll contact you when we go out hunting. Can you ask Cece and Tyson to be on call? We may need them." I stood, trying to quell the nausea that rose up when I saw the pictures.

"I will. Meanwhile, seeing what can happen..."

"We'll be careful. Trust me, Hank and Tad are far more cautious now, especially since Tad's stuck with a limp forever." I waved at her and, with one last look at the folder, I headed out. I wanted to stop in the library to find out the history of Devil's Gulch before I left for home.

CHAPTER SEVEN

THE GARRISON LIBRARY WAS THE ONLY PART OF CITY Central that was two stories. As I entered through the double doors, I crossed to the customer service desk. My friend, Charles Crichton, worked on the second floor. He was a member of the Moonshadow Bay Historical Society, and he was also a research librarian. It occurred to me that Charles might know more about the sluaghs, and that would be easier than trying to find out the history of the gulch.

"May I help you?" The librarian looked overworked and harried, but she still managed a smile.

"Is Charles Crichton in today?" It was always better to check with the main desk, in case he might be working on some project that he needed to focus on. He was so polite that he wouldn't hesitate to stop what he was doing, and I didn't like interrupting.

"Charles is in his office, yes. Would you like me to call him to see if he's available?"

"Thank you. Tell him January Jaxson's here and I'm wondering if he has a few minutes to help me out." I waited while she picked up the landline and punched a button.

A moment later, she rested the receiver back in the cradle. "Charles says for you to go right up to his office. Do you know where it is?"

"Yes, unless he's changed offices any time lately. Thank you," I said. I headed toward the elevator. A moment later, I was knocking on the door with his nameplate on it.

Charles opened it, ushering me in. A tall man—six-four if he was an inch—he was close to eighty, but his posture was straight and he was in good shape. He had smooth silver hair, neatly trimmed and slicked back, and he had on a pair of brown trousers and a lightweight sports jacket over a pale blue shirt. He had a wide smile and twinkling brown eyes.

"January, what a lovely surprise! Come in, please. Here, have a seat. Would you like some coffee? Water? I think I have a scone left, if you're hungry."

No one could ever accuse Charles of being impolite. "Thanks, I'm fine for now. It's good to see you, too, Charles. How have you been?" I didn't want to start off with an immediate request. I settled into the chair opposite him.

"It's been a difficult past couple years, actually. My lovely wife died. She was hit by a car while she was out on an evening stroll." His eyes dimmed and I could feel his sorrow.

I immediately prepared to leave. "I'm so sorry—I don't want to bother you. I'll go."

He let out a sad sigh. "No, please stay. It's been six months. It's still very difficult, but anything I can do to take my mind off of it helps. I've spent more time at work than I have in my home for the first time in years. It's so quiet there. We lost our cats a few years ago—they reached a dignified age. And now, the house echoes with memories that I can't face."

I wanted to hug him, but he seemed fragile, as if he'd shatter if I touched him. "I'm so sorry for your loss, Charles. Please, if you ever just want to talk, you can call me. We can go somewhere and have coffee or tea, and just...talk or sit in silence."

He adjusted his glasses. "Thank you. I may take you up on that. I can tell you stories about all the haunted houses and areas, and you can tell me about your ghost hunting. I think that would be a pleasant evening."

I pulled out my mini-planner, the one I kept in my purse. "What are you doing a week from tonight? Come over to dinner. You can meet my cats and husband, we can talk or watch a movie."

He seemed surprised. "Really? You mean it?"

"Of course. I like you, and I like talking to you. I should have invited you and your wife over before, but it's been a rough past year and I'm afraid I didn't have the spoons to go around. I've developed a chronic illness, and I am managing it but it was really hard in the beginning."

He nodded. "I'm sorry to hear that. If you want, feel free to talk about it, but I won't pressure you." He consulted his calendar. "I can make it on the fourth. Sevenish? Can you drink wine?"

"I can drink a little but it's better if I don't, given the herbs I'm on. But if you'd like to bring dessert—we're always open to a good dessert." I jotted down the note that Charles would be coming to dinner at seven P.M. on Saturday, May fourth.

"I make a mean tiramisu," he said.

"That sounds fantastic. Okay..." I took a deep breath. "I came in to ask if you might know anything about the sluagh. I need you to keep this quiet, please."

"Of course," Charles said. "I give you my word."

"Thanks, it's more important than you know. There's one loose around town and...through a long series of mishaps, it's up to me to destroy it."

"Ah, the sluagh. Well, January, if you're tasked with

destroying it, you're in for a rough fight. I'll need a little while to do some research. Can I call you tomorrow?" He jotted down a note on his notepad.

"Of course. That would be great. I should be off." I paused, then said, "I'm meeting one of the Fae tomorrow, Charles. I ended up having to ask him for a favor and now it's being called in—that's why I have to find and destroy the sluagh. Do you have any advice for me when I go talk to him?"

Charles slowly withdrew his glasses. "Oh, dear. That's a sticky wicket. All right, my best advice for you: think over everything you say before you say it."

"I know enough not to thank them," I said. "Is there any other phrase that might get me in trouble, besides 'Can you help me?' "

Charles stared at me for a moment. "My dear, the only advice I can give in good conscience is to skip the meeting. But I also understand that, if summoned, you must attend. Be aware of every word that comes out of your mouth. Listen to every word the Fae says. Every single word can be nuanced and have multiple meanings. Go and may the gods be with you. And I will see you at seven on the fourth. Thank you, for humoring a lonely old man."

"I'm not humoring you, and you might be older and lonely, but you're far more than that." I paused, then added, "Would you be offended if I gave you a hug?"

His face crinkled, his lips turning up for the first time in our talk. His eyes were watery. "I think I'd like that," he said.

I stepped around his desk and gave him a gentle hug, and while he was cautious in returning it, I could feel the need for touch, the need for a hug or a kiss. I leaned up and gently kissed his cheek. "We'll see you a week from tonight. Call me if you need directions, but it's easy to find. I'll text you the address." I gathered my things and left.

BY THE TIME I GOT HOME, IT WAS TIME TO PREPARE
dinner.

I cleared off the dining room table—that's where we held
our game nights. Then I pulled out all the ingredients that I'd
prepared that morning and began to assemble the lasagna. I
glanced at the clock. It was five, and they were supposed to
be here by seven. I tucked the lasagna back in the fridge,
covered with clear plastic cling. I'd take it out at five-thirty
and pop it in the oven at six. It would be piping hot and ready
by the time they arrived.

Next, I prepared the lemon poundcake mix. While it was
baking, I tossed the blueberries in a pot with some sugar and
lemon, and began to slowly simmer it so that it reduced. The
compote came together without a problem. Finally, I poured
it into a dish and set it in the fridge. By then, the cake was
done and I turned the loaf pan over, sliding the poundcake
out of the tin. I set it on a rack on the counter and slid the
lasagna in the oven. *Food prep, done*.

I was just finishing up with the cake when Killian came
through the kitchen door. He caught me up in his arms and
kissed me, then sniffed.

"It smells heavenly in here. Ooo, cake!" He reached for
the poundcake and I smacked his hand.

"Not till dinner. Hey, I haven't had a chance to clean up
yet. Can you set the table while I go change clothes?"

"Sure," he said, kissing me again. "Go. Change. But hurry,
so I can change too."

I dashed into our bedroom and slipped out of my
clothes, taking a couple moments to rinse off under the
shower, then slid into a pair of palazzo pants and a silky
tank top. It was a matching set—cobalt blue with gold and
black geometrical designs. I fixed my makeup and brushed

my hair back, and settled on a pair of silver satin block-heel slides.

As I entered the kitchen, Killian whistled. "You look good enough to eat." His eyes twinkled as he added, "Maybe that can be arranged later?"

I winked at him. "Sounds good. But for now, go get gussied up for your sister and her husband."

"Gussied up? I don't live on the prairie, love."

"No, but I like the word," I said, grinning as he took off for the bedroom.

Killian had set the table and placed a netted hood over the cake and compote to keep the cats out. Lemon pound-cake or fish sticks, Klaus tried to eat it all. We had to watch him around human food. I opened the bottom drawer of the sideboard and brought out a stack of board games. We usually stuck with two or three each game night, but it was always nice to have a choice. The timer went off on the stove and as I turned it off, the doorbell rang. After I took the lasagna out and set it on the table, I answered the door.

"Tally, Les, come on in."

"It smells wonderful," Tally said, giving me a hug. She wasn't as tall as Killian, but she was athletic. She was shorter than her brother, lanky and lean. Her hair was light brown and her eyes were also green. She had angular features that seemed almost sharp, and her movements were fluid—she was as graceful as she was in wolf form.

Les was the opposite. He had dark hair that hung to his shoulders, and vivid, dark eyes that gleamed with gold flecks. He had been the assistant to the Pack's shaman until they moved here, and even though he had given up the mantel of the job, he still radiated shifter magic. The shamans were the few magical members of the Packs, and they were both highly feared and respected. Les was as lean and lanky as Tally, though, which gave him a hungry look.

He, too, gave me a hug and a grunt, then headed over toward the table. "Ooo, you came through on the lasagna. You're the best sister-in-law, ever!"

Tally followed him, her eyes on the food. "I never seem to eat enough lately. Victoria and Leanna keep me so busy following them that I never have time to sit down. Thank gods for my mother." She reluctantly left the table and came over to sit by me in the living room. "Did I tell you that I got a job as manager of the Red Rock Café?"

"No, when did that happen?" The Red Rock Café was a new restaurant that had opened up down by the shore. It was somewhere between a diner and a fast-food joint, but the food was good and the décor was pleasant enough.

"I just got the call yesterday," she said. "I start in a week. That gives me time to prepare. I'm only working twenty-five hours a week. I wanted to pay Mom for her time. She told me under no circumstances is she charging me, but I don't want her helping out for free. I finally agreed, but we're planning on buying her a monthly gift certificate to a day spa. A standing monthly appointment."

I knew how expensive that was going to be, especially since Les and Tally were on a tight budget. "What about if Killian and I help you out on that? We can afford it, and they've done a lot of nice things for us, too. We can go half on the gift certificate and make it a full day of beauty for her." If Killian or I made the arrangements, we could get away with telling Les and Tally that it cost less than it did, and not wound their pride.

Tally glanced at Les. He caught my gaze and I realized he knew what I was doing, but he just smiled and nodded.

"I think that's a great idea, honey. Thanks, January, for wanting to be part of it," he said, sitting opposite her. I brought ice and sparkling water to the table and began to pour all around as Killian appeared.

Tally jumped up to hug him, and Les gave him a hearty handshake. As we gathered at the table for dinner, I realized this was what it felt like to have some sense of normalcy in a family. I felt it now and then, like when we hosted Thanksgiving, but not often. Then again, what constituted a normal family? The answer was: family looked different to everybody. No single definition worked for all.

Shrugging, I stopped thinking for the evening and began dishing out the lasagna. As we fell to eating, I told them about going back to work and we settled into comfortable dinner conversation.

BY EIGHT-THIRTY, I HAD JUST WON MY SECOND GAME OF Trivial Pursuit—thanks to my ever-present curiosity—when my phone rang. I glanced at the caller ID. It was Val.

"Go ahead and play. I need to take this," I said. I moved to the living room so I wouldn't disturb them as they shifted over to Scrabble. "Hey, Val," I said, curling up on the couch as I answered the call.

"Hey, yourself. Okay, I have information."

"Let me guess: the sluagh is in Devil's Gulch?"

Val sputtered. "What on earth gave it away?"

"A murder," I said. "Millie called me this morning."

Val grunted. "Well, then that lines up with what I found. I sent a couple of my men out. They damned near didn't come back. They got word through the grapevine that there was something going on in the gulch and so they went to check it out. Sure enough, there's something there and it's deadly. I'm guessing, by their description and by yours, it's the sluagh. By the way, if you would tell that damned Fae dandy that he needs to keep a tighter rein on his underlings—"

I snorted. "Not on your life. *You* tell him, if you want to chew him out. I've learned the hard way just how frightening the Fae are and I'm in no hurry to make enemies."

"Woman, you stab me in the heart," Val said, laughing. "Okay, so what I *can* tell you is that, though the gulch runs for several blocks, the creature seems to have made its lair near a culvert smack in the middle of the ravine. You won't notice it at first, but if you pinpoint where the runoff meets Devil's Creek, you'll find it. Be cautious, though," he said, his voice sobering. "The creature is more powerful than I think you realize."

I could hear the danger through his voice. Part of me wished that his men had taken it out themselves, but I fully understood that they didn't want to get involved in Fae politics. That was never a good thing. "Thanks, Val. Did your men actually have to fight it?"

"January, the minute they saw it, they ran. And you know my men, my people—vampires—we don't run from much. The sluagh seems to have an aura that stirs up fear and it works on vampires. They couldn't get out of there fast enough."

I thanked him and hung up. We knew where it was, now we just had to prepare to destroy it. As I dwelled on the thought, I returned to the dining room where Killian had just won the game. Talley was two points behind him, and Les, forty behind both.

"Who was it?" Killian asked.

"Oh, just a friend," I said. Right now, just for tonight, I didn't want to think about the task in front of us, or the hazards if we failed. I accepted a tile rack and picked seven tiles to start with as we started a new game, but my mind was far away, in the depths of Devil's Gulch, wondering just how hard this was going to be.

CHAPTER EIGHT

THE NEXT MORNING I WAS NERVOUS. I WAS SUPPOSED TO meet Briar to give him an update, and seeing the Fae Lord was the last thing I wanted to do. Charles called. He had emailed me all the notes he could find about the sluagh. I thanked him, told him we'd see him next week, then hung up and checked my email. Unfortunately, there wasn't much in his notes that I didn't already either know, or that I could use.

Killian was out back, mowing the lawn. He mowed his parents' lawn too, though it was small given we'd only sold them a small part of the backyard, keeping the rest of the land for ourselves. But he liked being able to do things for them, and I didn't complain about the extra time he spent there.

I stared at myself in the mirror. I wasn't sure what I was looking for, but I wanted everything to be just right when I met Briar. My hair was neatly pulled back in a ponytail, and I was dressed in a V-neck jersey top with three-quarters sleeves. It was lightweight, hunter green, and comfortable, yet it looked nice. I had paired it with a black gauze skirt and a pair of walking sandals. I added hoop earrings and my makeup was a little overdone, but it made me feel more confident. I checked my purse. My phone, a notebook, my on-the-go meds for my headaches, a bottle of water in the side pocket of the leather tote, keys, and wallet were all there.

"I guess I'm ready," I murmured. Briar had asked me to forge deep into the woodland. Well, probably a twenty-minute walk. He'd be at a crossroads, waiting for me. "Okay, don't be nervous. Nervous never won any awards."

I wanted to take somebody along with me, but Briar had said to come on my own, so I decided to follow directions, get in there, hear him out, and get out again while I was still safe.

I picked up the maple walking stick that Killian had carved for me. He dabbled in woodworking, and the staff wasn't the first one he'd made. It was golden brown, smooth, and splinterless. The handgrip was leather, as was the loop at the top of the stave. The handgrip was fastened to the wood by bronze grommets.

"Okay, let's get this over with," I said. I turned and made my way out of the bedroom, into the kitchen. It was time to go.

THE MYSTIC WOOD WAS ALIVE WITH ENERGY. THE NATURE spirits were out to play, I could tell, and the Woodlings were active. I'd grown used to their energy and though I seldom caught a glimpse of them, I knew they were around. It rankled me that they were slaves to the Fae, but it wasn't in my power to change that, and the Fae world wasn't my world.

Killian paused in his mowing as I stopped on my way toward the Mystic Wood. "Hey love, I'm going in."

"I wish you would let me go with you," he said, his eyes shining. His wolf was close to the surface, I could feel it.

Shaking my head, I said, "I wish you could come, but I don't think Briar would be pleased."

I was the first to admit that I was afraid. Every thread of common sense was telling me not to go, but the truth was, I had to show up. The Fae did not deal lightly. Bargains were sacred to them, and when I made a promise, I showed up to seal the deal. Briar had helped us, more than I expected, and I had given him a vow. As Judge Judy was fond of saying, you can't eat the steak and then refuse to pay. And we had eaten the steak.

Killian held my hands for a moment, then kissed me soundly. "If you're not back soon, Briar will have me to deal with, and an angry wolf is a dangerous wolf."

"No doubt," I whispered, leaning against his chest. "All right, I'd best get moving."

As I headed for the trailhead, I glanced back. Killian was watching me carefully. I blew him a kiss, then vanished into the thicket.

THE MOMENT YOU ENTERED THE MYSTIC WOOD, YOU could tell that you were in the depths of magic. The forest's heartbeat thundered through the woodland. Silent but vibrant, it reverberated with every leaf falling from the trees, with every hush as the wind played through the branches. The heart of the forest permeated everything that lived within, every stone, root, or blade of grass. And now, the lifeblood of the forest entwined around me, my heart matched its heart, and I, too, became a living avatar of the woodland.

I took the main path to a fork in the road, which veered to the left, deeper into the thicket. I was silent on the dusty path. The soil was compacted, but given there had been little rain lately, the dirt had loosened a bit and a light powder rose as I steadily followed the path.

The walking stick Killian had made for me was handy in more than one way. Besides offering a steadying force, I used it to bring down any spiders crossing my path, to push aside brambles so I could navigate around them, and to tap on the detritus that carpeted the forest floor. The woods in western Washington were cushioned with layers of leaves, tree needles, fir cones, and brambles that had built up over the years and it was easy to twist an ankle if you stepped into it wrong.

After about ten minutes, I came to two trees that over-stretched the path. Their branches were entwined, but the trees themselves looked like dead wood. But that was yet another illusion. The trees were alive and buzzing with energy. Witchblood could feel it, and so could others with the Sight.

I paused by the side, waiting for a moment. Then, after cycling around, the faint lines of a web showed up in the center. The lines were glowing, and I waited as they cycled through a series of colors, starting with red and moving through the chakra hues to indigo. I wasn't sure when to cross through, or if it would make any difference, but as I watched, the cycle shifted and swung around for the second time. Taking a deep breath, I decided there was no time like the present. Procrastinating wouldn't do any good. I exhaled, plunging through the portal, hoping it wouldn't lead to my ruin.

PORTALS IN THE MYSTIC WOOD LED TO YET MORE AREAS IN the Mystic Wood, ones that you wouldn't find by simply strolling through the forest. This portal opened into a clearing near a large knoll, tall enough to be a small hill. The mound was as tall as a two-story house, and it spread out to cover an acre of ground at the least. As I stared at it, a shimmer appeared on one edge of the hillock and the next thing I knew, Briar stepped through the side of the mound.

Well, that's different, I thought. I cleared my throat, straightened, and waited for him to walk over to me. I hadn't realized there were faerie mounds in the Mystic Wood.

He was as gorgeous as I remembered, tall and lanky with long black hair and ice blue eyes ringed with blacker-than-ink liner. Or at least it looked like he was wearing guyliner. For all I knew, it was the way he was born. His chiseled features were set in alabaster skin, and his lips were full and lush. All in all, he combined the beauty of Jack Sparrow with the intensity of Marilyn Manson.

He was wearing a pair of indigo-colored jeans and an olive-green poet's shirt that laced up the front. The laces were open at the top, showing a hint of his chest. He had on black leather boots that reminded me of a higher-heeled motorcycle boot, and a gold hoop shimmered off one of his slightly pointed ears.

"You came," he said.

"You summoned me. I owe you a debt. So here I am." I didn't want to say anything that might get me in trouble, so I had decided to stick to answering exactly what he said or asked.

"Walk with me." He motioned for me to follow him, and so I did. We walked past the barrow and I was surprised to find a rose garden beyond. It was well tended, with benches scattered here or there through the multitude of roses. The flowers were everywhere, hundreds of bushes in every color I could think of. Even though it wasn't quite May, the temperature felt warmer here, and the bushes were all out in full bloom. I stopped short when I saw a true blue rose.

"Oh," I said, staring at it.

"You like this?" Briar asked, reaching out to stroke the petals.

I nodded. "We don't really have blue roses. The color doesn't exist in the rose family. How do you grow them?"

"We have our magic," Briar said, picking off one of the roses and handing it to me.

I lifted it to my nose. The scent of rose was overlaid with the scent of something else. I couldn't identify it, but it smelled like dusky summer nights and moonlit walks. I started to thank him but caught myself.

"This is beautiful," I said, staring at the rose.

"Please, sit." He motioned to a nearby bench and I gingerly took my seat.

Briar sat near me, but not close enough to make me uncomfortable. "So, how is the search for the sluagh faring?"

"Well, I think I know where it's hiding. And I've learned several things about its nature." Before I could stop myself, I added, "It would have helped if you would have given me a dossier on it, you know."

Briar grinned—a slow, easy grin that caught me off guard. "Ah, but where's the fun in that? You're a *tenquitara*, you should be able to find out these things."

"I'm a witch, but that doesn't mean I have access to all the documents in the world. But I do know that it's going to be a battle fighting the sluagh. They're dangerous. It's already killed two of our townsfolk and injured a third." I shook my head. "How did it get loose? Do your people—the Overkings —keep control over all of the sub-Fae?"

Briar sprawled against the back of the bench. He was cocky, arrogant in the way people have when they're born and bred to not only think, but *know*, that they're better than others.

"Eventually, if negotiations go right, you'll know more

about us. We need to enter the ways of the world, even to a minor degree, and the best way to make that entrance is to work with witchblood. And so, we negotiate for an even footing on which to do so." He straightened. "If negotiations falter, there will be trouble."

I stared at him. He was deadly serious now. "Trouble? Like what?"

"Just hope that the negotiations conclude successfully. We're in the later stages but until we strike the bargain, anything can upset the cart."

"Does my grandmother know about all of this?" I was truly curious. She hadn't said a thing to me.

"Yes, but you are not to question her. She won't give you an honest answer, because she's not allowed to, regardless of your familial connections. But back to the sluagh. You say you know where it is? And it's truly neither male nor female. They're hermaphroditic, and they can reproduce without a mate. Hence, you'd better capture it before it spawns eggs, because it can fertilize them as well. And be aware, bullets will not work against them. Only cold iron."

I blinked. "That's not good. And yes, I think we know where to find it. I'm going to call my coworkers and, hopefully, go hunting for it this afternoon. Now that I know it can reproduce on its own, there's a time crunch. The last thing we want is for more of them to be running around." I paused, then decided to ask a question I'd been thinking about. "This *will* take care of my debt, I assume?"

Briar gazed into my eyes and I could feel him pulling me in, so I turned my head, studying the vast array of roses around me.

"Do you want it to?" he said softly.

"Quit toying with me," I said, keeping my gaze focused on the rose in my hand. The tea I had drunk was kicking in. I could now feel the charm he was working on me, and I could resist it.

After a moment, he let out an exasperated sigh. "Then yes, it will. Destroy the sluagh and you are free from your obligations."

I almost said *thank you*, but once again, caught myself. I shook my head as I stood.

"How the human world is going to manage interacting with the Fae, I have no clue. I just hope the negotiations include a damper on those little ways you have of entrapping people into unintentional obligations. Anyway, if you have nothing more to say to me, about the sluagh or anything else, I'll be going." I stood. "Oh, when I've managed to destroy it, should I send word through Rebecca?"

Briar looked none too pleased, but nodded. "That will work. I'll see you again, I hope. Allow me to walk you back to the portal and help you through."

Again, I refused to thank him, merely nodded. He walked me back to the pair of trees and, without a word, I stepped through them and back into my world. I let out a sigh of relief to see Rebecca there, standing beside a large lovely gray wolf.

I knelt beside the wolf, throwing my arms around his shoulders. "You were worried about me!" The wolf nuzzled my neck, then licked my face as he searched my eyes. "I'm all right," I said. "Honest. It wasn't that pleasant but..." I paused, then looked down at the rose in my hand. It shimmered in the forest light, and then vanished into a wisp of blue smoke, as though it had never been there.

Rebecca, chatting about the weather, guided us back to the trailhead, where she slipped into the bushes. Killian and I walked back to the house together, where he changed back into his human form.

I told him what had happened. "I need to call the others. It's imperative we catch this thing now, before it lays eggs."

"I agree, on one condition," Killian said.

"What's that?"

"I'm coming with you and the others. You're not going into Devil's Gulch without me."

And this time, I couldn't find a reason to say no.

CHAPTER NINE

T<small>AD AND THE OTHERS WERE ALREADY AT THE OFFICE WHEN</small> Killian and I showed up. Hank was sorting out several weapons I had never seen—it wasn't like we kept much in the way of weaponry at work. But we'd need them to go after the sluagh. On the way over, I'd informed Millie that we were going to take care of the creature and could they be ready if we needed them. Since bullets wouldn't work against the sluagh, I didn't want the officers going in expecting they could take it down that way.

Hank spread out what he had been able to gather. There were two crowbars, a couple of daggers, a crossbow and a quiver of bolts, and he held up what looked like a blowgun.

"A blowgun? Really?"

He nodded. "I know how to use it, and I've fit it with iron darts. I've added a tincture of iron to the needles, so that it will get into the creature's bloodstream. The trouble with this is that I have to be at a certain distance. So I can't be upfront to fight it. I'll need to be back a ways."

Killian shook his head. "I'm going with you in my wolf form. I can grapple it that way, and while it might be strong and dangerous, so am I when I let my full wolf out. You know wolf shifters are stronger than the animals we belong to."

Tad nodded. "I always thought so. Then you can go in the lead. I'm not good for much fighting, not with a bum leg, but I can use the crossbow. I can shoot from a distance too."

"I'll go in my bobcat form," Caitlin said. "I can leap from a tree limb and surprise it."

"I wish we could just blow it up," I said. "Millie will meet us there with the cops, but she can't officially ask them to destroy it until it puts one of us in danger. So I'll have to engage as much as I can. I'm glad you left Wren in the dark. She'd want to be here, and that wouldn't be a good thing." I worried my lip. "I guess I'll take one of the crowbars. What magic I've got won't work against the creature."

"We'd better get going, then. I also have three daggers with iron blades," Hank said. He handed one to me, one to Tad, and kept one for himself. "Let's go. We definitely can't let the sluagh breed."

And with that, sans our usual gear, which would do no good at all, we headed for the van. Killian disrobed in the bathroom, as did Caitlin in the powder room, and I packed their clothes in two bags after they emerged in their wolf and bobcat forms.

"I guess we're ready," I said, not feeling ready at all. But I wanted this over and done with as soon as possible, and so we headed for the van. Tad drove, while the rest of us sat in pensive silence as we made our way to Devil's Gulch.

DEVIL'S GULCH WAS A DARK, FOREBODING PART OF THE Mystic Wood. Near the southern edge of town, the surrounding neighborhood was weathered. While you couldn't call it a slum by any sense of the word, the houses were definitely not affluent.

The gulch itself stretched the length of four city blocks, and the undergrowth in the deep ravine was thick and difficult to navigate. There were a few trails running through the gulch, but they, too, were overgrown and seldom touched. The city wouldn't send workers out to clean up the gulch unless there was a reason, and that reason had to be important enough to convince the crews to enter the dark thicket.

Even when I was little, I remembered my mother forbidding me to walk through the gulch because there were too many dark spirits and deeds attached to it. There had been one incident where a child molester had managed to hide out there for two weeks before police caught him. They found the abducted child near him, inside a tent, but the young boy was dead and so the charges were upped to murder. But before he ever made it to court, the perv offed himself in jail.

My mother had muttered, "Good riddance to bad rubbish," when she heard. But even though he had been caught, she cautioned me against going there anyway because of both the potential for spirits and the thought that if one freak had chosen to hide out there, another could easily do the same.

Tad pulled into the turnout that led down into one of the main trails winding through the ravine. "Here we are. The culvert isn't far from here—about half a block to our north. We should have some sort of plan going in."

"We use me as bait so Caitlin and Killian can distract it while you and Hank shoot it," I said. "That's the best idea I can think of."

Killian raised his hackles and growled. I leaned down and wrapped my arms around his head, kissing him on the muzzle.

"I'm sorry, but that's just the way it's got to be," I told

him. "We have to draw it out and since I'm the most likely-looking potential victim, I'll go in first. Just make sure you're close enough to start shooting. I'll try to get out of the way so do your best to avoid shooting me, please." I stared down the sides of the ravine. "Crap, that's not an easy hike. I'm glad I wore walking shoes and jeans." I'd changed clothes before we headed out for the office.

"We'll make sure you're okay," Hank said. He held my gaze and I realized that this was his chance to make amends to Tad and me, and he was counting on it.

"I trust you," I said. "All right, let's go in."

I led the way over to the edge and after a moment to scan the sides, I picked out the easiest route downward. I set foot over the edge and, using my walking stick, began to ease my way down the sides.

The footing was slick, but manageable. The soil wasn't dry yet. We still had so much spring moisture in the air, and the rain would return several more times before summer arrived, but at least it wasn't a mudhole all the way down.

I slowly inched my way along the slope in a downward direction, angling myself so that I wasn't trying to hike straight down toward the bottom. Moving sideways made the descent easier and I gnawed on my lip as I zigzagged my way toward the bottom. It took me more than ten minutes, though if I was better at the descent, I might have been at the bottom in just a few.

Finally, after slipping a few times and almost rolling down the hill, I managed to step off the slope and onto the shore next to the creek. I waited while the others followed me down. Killian was first, and was at my side within minutes, as was Caitlin, who came soon after. Hank took longer, because he was helping Tad. Finally, they made it down.

The walking space on either side of the creek was narrow, but it was wide enough for us to form a single-person line and file through the ferns and skunk cabbage that filled the cushioned floor. The water was running high, but the creek wasn't all that wide. If I fell in the creek, I'd be fine. Wet and cold, but all right.

Another five minutes of steady walking brought the culvert into sight. It was on the other side of Devil's Creek, and the open end overflowed with water pouring into the stream. The moment I saw it, I slowed and began to scan the area, looking for the sluagh. Although we had a description—several, in fact—having never laid on this creature in person put us at a disadvantage.

The sluagh was nowhere in sight, and my first thought was that it was probably wandering through the woods, looking for victims. I turned to the others and motioned to the culvert.

"I want to look inside to see what I might be able to find. It might have a nest in there, though with the water running through the culvert, that's unlikely. But better to check it out and know for sure."

Killian tried to tug on my sleeve, but I patted him on the head. "I know what I'm doing."

A series of stones crossed the stream near the culvert that could be used as stepping stones. I set my foot on the first, and—using the walking stick to brace me against the slippery moss covering the stones and the water rushing over them—I began to pick my way across the creek. Killian followed behind me. I knew he was worried, but I had to check the culvert.

I stepped onto the opposite side of the creek, followed by Killian. Hank crossed next, then Caitlin. Tad wasn't balanced enough, so he stayed where he was, prepping the crossbow.

I stared at the pipe jutting out over the stream. It was several feet off the ground—too high for me to pull myself up. I glanced at Hank, but he had his blowgun out and was messing with it. And I didn't want to tie him up, just in case the sluagh was inside after all.

Looking around, I noticed a large chunk of wood. It was part of an old tree stump. I asked Hank to help me wrestle it over to the culvert and, once we had it in place, he stepped back while I balanced on top of it.

The culvert was a good five feet in diameter. The stump was high enough that I managed to drag myself up, bracing my hands on the sides of the pipe while kneeling in the flowing water. The force was almost enough to knock me into the stream, but I held tight long enough to turn on a flashlight. I placed the handle in my mouth, hoping I wouldn't bite down and hurt my teeth. I looked ridiculous, but it was the only way I could think of to get a look inside.

The pipe went straight back into the dirt, and from what I could see, there was nothing inside except for piles of sodden leaves against the bottom, beneath the water. I waited for a moment, then managed to drop back down to the ground.

"Not in there, and I doubt it has been. The culvert goes into the hill, straight back as far as the light would reach, and there's nothing to indicate that anything living has been in there." I looked around. "I wonder where..."

I froze. Caitlin was staring at a spot in the undergrowth, and Killian suddenly went on the defensive, his hackles rising, and he growled, low and deep.

"What do we have here," I said softly.

Hank immediate readied his blowgun as I began to walk slowly in the direction Killian and Caitlin were facing. The ferns were waist high in the undergrowth, and several huckleberry bushes rose to overcrowd the side of the ravine.

The next moment, all hell broke loose as the sluagh broke free from where it was hiding and came barreling in my direction. I screamed and, without a thought, brought up the crowbar, swinging it wildly. I missed as the sluagh darted to the side.

"Fuck!" Still startled, I stumbled back, catching my shoe on the side of the streambed. I flailed, trying to regain my balance, then went toppling backward into the water.

The sluagh followed suit, landing in the water with me. It was hideous—its torso blending directly into its head without any sign of a neck. Its huge, single eye was cold and black, and the body was an odd bluish color. It had arms and legs, but they were as spindly as the torso was thick.

I had lost the crowbar but I still had the dagger and I yanked it out of my belt as I managed to roll over and get on all fours. The rocks on the bottom of the streambed were slippery, and I knew that I wouldn't be able to stand on them without losing my balance—the current was too swift and the sluagh, too close. Even though the stream wasn't very high, I could still drown if the creature caught hold of me and pulled me under. I fumbled with the dagger, holding it out in front of me as the sluagh turned my way. It was growling, and the needle-sharp teeth looked dangerously sharp. Its single eye gleamed at me with a fetid light.

Hank shouted from the bank, but I couldn't focus on what he was saying. All I could focus on was keeping track of where the sluagh was as it headed toward me, through the water.

There was a thudding sound as a large dart hit the sluagh in the side. It let out a gurgling scream, then sort of stretched and leapt in one motion, landing directly in front of me like a frog.

I tried to steady myself, holding out one arm as I raised the other, clutching my dagger. I brought it down toward the sluagh, but as I leaned forward, I slipped and landed in the water again, this time gashing my chin on a rock.

"Motherfu—" I started, but stopped as I realized the

sluagh was face to face with me. I had visions of Ripley and the alien as the sluagh's eyes lit up and it snapped at me. I jerked back, but it caught my shoulder and those razor-sharp teeth bit deep, plunging into my flesh.

The next moment, there was a wolf in the mix. Killian joined the fray, and he growled, howling loudly as he loped through the water to grab one of the sluagh's feet in his teeth. His attack threw the creature off and it turned to see who had hold of it.

I took that moment to bring the dagger down against the sluagh's shoulder. The blade bit, sliding into its flesh, and a hissing sound told me I'd hit paydirt. The sluagh screamed as the iron began to boil against it, and the flesh sizzled.

As it fell back away from me, taking the dagger with it, I frantically scrambled for the crowbar. *Any port in the storm.* Unfortunately, I'd dropped it when I first fell in the stream and it was nowhere in sight.

Killian yanked on the sluagh's legs, biting so hard that the sluagh floundered, falling forward. Caitlin leapt on its back, raking at it with her claws.

I shouted for Hank and Tad to shoot as I pulled back. Both let loose—Tad with an arrow and Hank with his blow-gun. And both hit. The arrow pierced the creature's shoulder as the dart landed straight into its forehead. The iron sizzled as it pierced its skin.

Still, the sluagh fought on. It turned and landed one fist against Killian's muzzle and the wolf let out a yelp, letting go of the creature's leg. Caitlin began clawing furiously on the sluagh's back and it twisted, trying to throw her off.

At that moment, Tad shot another arrow and this time, it found solid purchase, piercing cleanly into the sluagh's side. Once again, the creature let out a terrible shriek and it bucked, throwing Caitlin off into the water. The bobcat loped across the stream and landed on the shore.

I was nearing the shore now, fighting the slippery rocks beneath my feet, when the sluagh suddenly made another beeline for me, fury in its dark eyes. Its mouth wide open, it aimed its rows of needle-sharp teeth directly at me. I jumped, landing on the shore, and tried to roll out of the way but the sluagh landed on top of me, the arrow still lodged in its side.

I grappled at the soaking wet creature, but it was far heavier than it looked and it had me pinned. It made a mad rush for my face and I turned my neck, whipping my head from side to side as I managed to miss being skewered by those teeth. As it reared back for another attempt, I grabbed hold of the arrow and tried to shove it in deeper.

Another second and there was another weight atop me when Killian landed on top of both of us. He dug his teeth deep into the sluagh's shoulder. I winced as it shrieked and blood sprayed all over me from the wound. Killian held on, trying to drag it off me, as Caitlin joined in. She bit it on the top of the head as she helped Killian pull it away. They managed to drag it off me as Hank ran up, dagger in hand. As Killian and Caitlin held the thrashing sub-Fae to the ground, Hank brought the dagger down, digging deep into its torso.

I sat up, panting, aching everywhere. But the sluagh convulsed and, as the light faded from its eye, I realized we'd managed to take it down. It shivered again, then collapsed. Killian and Caitlin held tight to it until it ceased to move. Killian gave it another shake, but it was limp and lifeless. As he and Caitlin let go, I brought my knees up to my chest, breathing deeply. The sub-Fae was dead, and I was free from my debt.

The body of the sluagh began to bubble, melting into a pile of goo that soaked into the ground. It was over.

CHAPTER TEN

MILLIE WAS ABLE TO UNOFFICIALLY CLOSE THE CASE ON Dwayne Stephens and the other murder victim, so that was one headache off her books. Although there wasn't any proof it had ever existed, she made notes in the file and tucked it away into a folder she kept for the cases that were unexplained on paper, but that she knew were done and over with.

There was nothing left of the creature, and I hoped that it hadn't had time to make a nest or lay eggs, but we'd have to wait and see about that.

I had managed to get a picture of the creature's corpse before it vanished, and I printed it out and wrote out a note to Briar telling him we were done and that the case was over. I folded the picture and tucked it into the envelope, wrote Briar's name on it, then handed it to Rebecca.

She took the envelope, glancing up at me. "Congratulations."

"Just so long as I'm done dealing with the Overkings," I said.

"I don't like them much myself," she said. "They're too powerful for their own good."

I wondered what was going on with the negotiations, and I wasn't entirely sure whether I hoped they'd be successful or not. I still thought it was dangerous to allow the Fae loose on human society—there was far too much danger for misunderstandings. But it wasn't my place to say so.

After a trip to urgent care—I was covered with bruises and needed four stitches in my chin to sew up the gash, and a hefty dose of antibiotics given the sluagh had bitten me—Killian, shifting back to being human, drove me home. I snuggled on the sofa with the cats while he made us cocoa and cookies and texted Ari.

YOU KNOW BRIAR? I FULFILLED MY DEBT AND THAT'S NOW OFF THE TABLE.

A moment later, she texted back. THAT'S GOOD NEWS—I DIDN'T LIKE HIM HAVING A HOLD ON YOU. Another moment and she texted me again. WHAT ABOUT COFFEE TOMORROW? I THOUGHT YOU MIGHT LIKE TO SEE THE KIDS. COME OVER TO OUR HOUSE AFTER WORK.

I hesitated, then texted, ARE YOU SURE?

THEY MISS YOU, Ari texted back. AND *I* MISS YOU TOO. PLEASE COME VISIT.

ALL RIGHT, I'LL BE THERE AROUND FIVE, IF YOU'RE SURE.

I AM, she texted. SEE YOU THEN.

I set down my phone, feeling relieved in a way I could barely explain. The world was coming back into balance. We had neighbors we loved, we had new friends—Tally and Les—to hang out with, and old friends were coming back in the picture. Tad and Caitlin were getting married. I was working more magic and back at the job I loved. Best of all, Killian and the cats and I had settled into a happy family.

Life was good.

I knew it couldn't always stay this way. There were bound to be bumps, some large and some just blips on the radar, but for now, for the first time in my life, I belonged in a way that set my heart soaring. I turned on the TV, and we settled in for the best evening we could have—an evening to ourselves, snuggled together, healthy...and happy.

Read on for two bonus never before published short stories!

IF YOU LOVE ROMANTASY (FANTASY ROMANCE), ORDER the first book in the Winter's Spell Trilogy: WEAVING WINTER. After her mother's death, Asajia discovers that the sheriff is planning to confiscate her inheritance, and force her to join his harem. Rather than accept her fate, she escapes into the darkly enchanted Bramble Fel Forest—a forest cursed with the perpetual breath of Winter, nightmarish creatures, and dark, dangerous secrets. Asajia would rather take her chances with *real* monsters than submit to the vile man. But when his raiders finally track her down, her magic is too unpredictable to save herself, and she finds herself outnumbered with nowhere to run.

A band of outcast wolf shifters arrives just in time to rescue her, but Asajia finds herself caught between the charming Wolf Prince and his rogue assassin brother. There is only one thing Asajia knows for certain—the sheriff will never stop looking for her, so she has little choice but to put her trust in one of the warring brothers. Who will she choose?

For more of the Starlight Hollow Series, you can preorder Elphyra's next book. Together with her red dragonette—Fancypants—she both protects *and* heats up the town in every sense of the word. Preorder the fourth book, STARLIGHT WITCH, now! Begin the series with STARLIGHT HOLLOW.

For more of The Moonshadow Bay Series: January Jaxson returns to the quirky town of Moonshadow Bay after her husband dumps her and steals their business, and within days she's working for Conjure Ink, a paranormal investigations agency, and exploring the potential of her hot new neighbor. Twelve books are currently available. If you haven't read the other books in this series, begin with **Starlight Web**.

For all the rest of my current and finished series, check out my **State of the Series page**, and you can also check the Bibliography at the end of this book, or check out my website at **Galenorn.com** and be sure and sign up for my **newsletter** to receive news about all my new releases. Also, you're welcome to join my **YouTube Channel** community.

QUALITY CONTROL: This work has been professionally edited and proofread. If you encounter any typos or formatting issues ONLY, please contact me through my **website** so they may be corrected. Otherwise, know that this book is in my style and voice and editorial suggestions will not be entertained. Thank you.

CHAPTER ELEVEN

Tarvish's Kittens

(Bonus Moonshadow Bay scene that takes place between *Cursed Web* and *Solstice Web*)

"What do you mean, we can't get a kitten?" Tarvish asked. Disappointment made his voice shake to the point where Rowan turned around to stare at him. The Funtime demon wasn't having much fun right now, that was for sure.

"I just don't have the time to take care of one. And I've got so many poisonous plants in the greenhouse that I'd be afraid they'd get in there and hurt themselves." Rowan hated disappointing Tarvish. She was truly fond of him, although she couldn't exactly use the word *love*, but she cared for him and she knew how much he loved cats. He didn't ask for much, and he did his best to help around the house and the land.

"Oh," Tarvish said. He looked for a moment like he was going to argue, but then shrugged in an offhand way and turned back to his crossword puzzle. He seemed resigned to her decision, but Rowan had the sneaking suspicion that he was going to try again sometime soon.

ROWAN WAS OUT IN THE YARD, DEADHEADING THE FLOWERS and turning over the plants. The chill of the autumn afternoon buoyed her up, bracing her as the smell of wood smoke from neighboring houses drifted past. The pungent scent rising from the soil—petrichor—sour and yet comforting, whispered autumn's days were nearly done and winter was coming in.

She stood back, bracing herself on the pitchfork, as she stared around the garden. Rowan had been alive for a long time, but some days—like today—made her feel young again, in tune with the Earth and Her cycles. Autumn was Rowan's element, and fire was her power, and both reigned strong in her soul.

It occurred to her it would be fun to make a bonfire in the firepit, and roast hotdogs and marshmallows, and make s'mores. She made a mental note to call January, her granddaughter, and invite her and Killian, and January's aunt Teran, and a few other close friends to join them. The autumn had been overly busy, and they needed to celebrate now that the curse on January's family had been lifted.

Rowan stood there, contemplating what to work on next —it was either time to turn over the tomato plants (she had already collected the last of the green ones and wrapped them away to ripen), or she could cut down the cornstalks and shred them into the compost bin. Finally, she sucked in a deep breath of cool, crisp air and was about to tackle the tomatoes when she heard a faint cry coming from beneath a nearby azalea bush. Frowning, she walked over to the sprawling shrub. Once again she heard something—another faint cry. Kneeling, she peered beneath the latticed branches, trying to see what was making the noise.

"Oh, good grief. Just what we need."

As she reached beneath the bush, her gloved hand brushing away some of the deadwood, the first kitten hesitantly stumbled her way. As she took hold of it, gently bringing the tiny creature out to examine it, she saw that there were three other kittens beneath the azalea, and they all looked shaky and cold.

The one in her hand was a gray tuxedo, and two of the others looked to be silver tabbies. The fourth was what she called a cow kitten—with black and white patches.

The gray tuxi feebly pawed at Rowan, then tried to bury itself against her chest. She could feel its hunger, and its fear. As much as she knew there was no going back, she slid the kitten into her basket of broccoli, and then reached for the others. As soon as she had all four of them, she carried the pitchfork over to the tool rack and secured it, then—cradling the basket—Rowan headed inside.

THE KITCHEN SMELLED LIKE BANANAS AND CINNAMON. Tarvish had made banana bread, and he was reading the newspaper on his tablet as Rowan entered the room. Immediately, the kittens set up a loud caterwaul and Tarvish immediately set down his tablet and jumped up.

"I swear," Rowan said, trying to hide a grin. "You have some magic to make wishes come true, don't you?"

Tarvish laughed, his baritone echoing through the room. "*Where* did you find those? And no, I wish I did but I'm no djinn." He took the basket from her and immediately pulled out his phone. "I'll call Killian. It's Saturday and he should be off work today."

"I found them under the azalea bush. It's a good thing I was out there because if they were exposed to the elements much longer, I doubt they would have survived. I hope I found them in time." Even though she didn't want to deal with a house full of thundering kittens, Rowan was a soft-hearted woman, deep down. She *liked* cats, she just didn't have time to take care of them. "I wonder where their mother is. They seem awfully hungry."

"I think I know," Tarvish said softly. "Yesterday afternoon, I found a dead cat out on the road. She'd been hit by a car. I didn't see any collar or markings, so I buried her. She looked a little thin, so it didn't occur to me that she might be feeding kittens. But she looked a lot like these silver tabbies."

"That was probably their mother, poor thing. My intuition says so. You call Killian and watch them while I go find a blanket and a box to tuck them into." She paused. "And before you ask, *if* you take care of them—including the cat box and feeding them—we'll keep them. But they're all getting spayed and neutered, and you're going to have to help me catproof the house this weekend. Until then, we'll keep them in the second bath."

Tarvish put in a call to Killian, and within the hour both he and January were cooing over the kittens as Killian checked them out. The gray tuxi and the cow cat were boys, the silver tabbies were girls. They were all hungry and a little malnourished, and they had fleas, but they would survive.

Rowan decided they might as well have the bonfire dinner that night, so she called Teran to join them, and then January went grocery shopping while Killian and Tarvish played with the kittens and warmed them up, Rowan stood back and watched over her family.

For so long it'd been just her. Oh, she had her friends and she had the Crystal Cauldron, but until January had returned to Moonshadow Bay, Rowan had led a fairly solitary life.

Now, she had a significant other. While he was rather scary to look at, he was one hell of a lover and a devoted boyfriend. And she had her granddaughter January, and her granddaughter's fiancé. Rowan had even grown close to Teran, January's aunt. After well over a hundred years of living in relative solitude, Rowan's world was expanding. And now that world would be expanding to include four kittens.

Laughing softly, she turned to start kitten proofing the house. And surprisingly, she didn't mind it one bit.

CHAPTER TWELVE

The Green Faerie

(Bonus scene that takes place between Crystal **Web and Witch's Web)**

Teran stared at the green bottle of absinthe sitting on the counter. She let out a slow breath as she waited. She'd whispered the incantation, had sacrificed the crystal by grinding it to powder and sprinkling it at the base of the mandrake root, and now she was waiting for a sign. After half an hour, she decided that the spell was going to take more time than she wanted to wait around for, so she headed to her kitchen to grab a handful of chocolate chip cookies.

She was two cookies into the stack when a loud noise alerted her. Slowly, she placed the cookies on the counter and then jogged toward the greenhouse, which was affixed to the side of her house.

"I hope the neighbor cat didn't get into the greenhouse," she said to Prue as she hurried along.

Don't worry, you never let them have a chance, Prudence said. *They know better and they trust you when you tell them it's dangerous in there for them.*

Prue was her Lady—her aunt who had come knocking on

her spiritual door with the white rose when Teran was twenty-five. That had been almost half a century ago, and Prue had never let her down yet. Sometimes, Teran wondered what it would have been like to not live in a family where the matriarchy ruled and her female ancestors guarded over the living, but the thought made her shudder and she pushed it out of her mind.

As Teran entered the greenhouse, she glanced around, looking for any intruder. But her wards were strong and there were no invaders, be they from the astral plane or from her neighborhood. However, she did notice that the crystal dust on the soil surrounding the mandrake had vanished, and that the bottle of absinthe had divested itself of its cork—all on its own. The cork was on the floor, near one of the windows.

Bingo, she thought. *The spell took. Now to find her.*

Teran cautiously walked over to the bottle. When dealing with imps, one always had to be careful. The Green Faerie was well known in magical circles, though she wasn't a true faerie. She wasn't even a true imp. She was a spirit of the absinthe, which—for the purposes of Teran's earth magic— also translated into an oracle. And right now, Teran was looking for help.

A laugh echoed from one of the dwarf lemon trees growing on the far side of the greenhouse. Teran started toward it. For years she had worked on her greenhouse, slowly adding on to it each time she managed to get a chunk of spare change. Finally, when one of her CDs matured, she took the money and finished the final enlargement.

Now the greenhouse was spacious, almost half the size of her cottage, and since it was fully heated and protected from the elements, Teran had added a rocking chair and a small table in the corner, so she could relax in the greenhouse and spend time with her plants. Witchblood who worked with the earth element tended to feel strongest when they were surrounded by greenery.

Teran slowly approached the lemon tree. The laughter grew louder, not maniacal but with a wild and free tone.

"Who's there?" she said. She wasn't at all sure that anyone would reply, but after a moment a sultry voice echoed from behind the tree trunk.

"You *know* who I am. You summoned me."

"The Green Faerie? Is it really you?" Teran tried to get a glimpse of her but in the dim light, all she could see was a swirl of sparkles. Green and purple, with a hint of gold thrown in. They were mesmerizing, glittering like gems in the night.

There was a pause, and then, as if in slow motion, the Green Faerie appeared, stepping out from behind the tree trunk. She was as beautiful as Teran had imagined. The faerie had long black hair that sparkled with glints of light, as though it had been streaked with purple glitter. With golden skin, with almond-shaped eyes that were the most lustrous green Teran had ever seen, the creature was beautiful. Her wings were long and nebulous, as if made of smoke. A gossamer dress woven of spiderwebs trailed over her body, making her look more nude than if she had been wearing nothing.

"You summoned me. What do you want?" The faerie sauntered over toward Teran, stopping at the edge of the planter. Effortlessly, she spiraled into the air and glided over to sit beside Teran on the table.

Teran lowered herself into the rocking chair, doing nothing that might startle the Green Faerie and chase her off. "I have a boon to ask you. A favor for my niece."

"What do you need?" The Green Faerie looked bored. "I'm not a djinn, you know. I don't hand out wishes like candy to every witch who summons me."

It wasn't exactly the reaction Teran had hoped for, but she had been prepared for it. Working with the elementals and nature spirits was difficult enough. But working with a spirit from the realm of alcohol was another matter.

Teran had once met the spirit of tequila, and—after waking up from a twenty-hour hallucination fest—she swore she never wanted to deal with any of them again. But the Green Faerie could help January kickstart her work with herbs and spices. She could help her touch the very core of the element of Earth. Oh, January was already pledged to Druantia, a goddess of the earth. But that didn't mean that she had truly touched the core of earth magic itself.

"I have a niece," Teran said. "She's an earth witch come late to her element. I'd like to help her strengthen her connection with the earth, and the energy of the earth magic. I know that you can do that. I was wondering if you would be willing to help me."

"I can do that," the Green Faerie said. "But give me a good reason why I *should*, and remember, I'm not an altruistic soul." She sat, leaning back flat on the soil in the planter as she rested her arms under her head.

Teran thought it odd that the faerie wasn't afraid of her. After all, she was far larger, and she was a fairly powerful witch.

Just then, the Green Faerie sat up, staring at her. "Don't *ever* think you're stronger than I am," she said. "I can hear your thoughts as clearly as I can hear the clock ticking, as clearly as I can hear the wind blowing, as clearly as I can hear the worms crawling through the soil."

"I'm sorry—" Teran started to say but the Green Faerie cut her off.

"Don't ever make the mistake of thinking you're more powerful than I am, because I can destroy you. I could destroy your mind if I wanted to. I've done it before, and I'll do it again."

The faerie's words hit Teran to the core. She could feel the energy drifting off the creature, and now it hit her full force. She caught a glimpse of just how destructive the Green Faerie could be and it shook her bone-deep.

"I apologize. I was just surprised that..." Teran was well spoken, but she had no clue how to get out of this one. After a moment, she sighed and shrugged. "All I can say is I'm sorry. I meant nothing by it."

"Why didn't your niece start learning her magic from a young age?" the creature asked.

"Because her mother was stupid. I loved my sister, but she was hesitant about her own abilities, and so she placed her daughter in a precarious situation. January's lucky that she didn't implode from a buildup of residue power. That can happen to witchblood. January did try her best to teach herself, but her ex was a human who...was basically a giant cockroach. Now, she's trying to make up for lost time. She needs to learn the basics as quickly as she can."

There was a surge that all witches went through near their fifties, and it was accompanied by a great increase in power. If unprepared, it could scramble the brains or short out their natural instincts. So, the more prepared they were, the better they weathered the storm.

"You really do need help." The faerie stood, dusting off the back of her gossamer dress. "And you know that my way is not gentle. What I can do isn't a pat on the back."

"I know, and I'll warn her first. But we don't have time for methods that can reprogram her mindset. My instinct is urging me to help her through this now. I don't know why, but it feels important. So, will you help me?"

"I suppose. But in repayment, I want a year of your life.

One year. No more, no less." The faerie gave Teran a long look, waiting for an answer.

Teran hung her head. She had done enough research to know what the Green Faerie was capable of, and that she would ask a huge payment in return. But Teran *also* knew she had already beaten the odds. The women in her family died young thanks to a curse, and Teran had lived longer than she had expected to. She wasn't looking forward to dying, but there was some comfort in knowing that at least, when *she* did go, she would've helped her niece in a way that few others except those of witchblood could.

"All right. I agree." Teran held out her hand and the faerie pressed her own fingers against Teran's palm.

"The deal is done. I will create the elixir for you. And the ritual to go with it. It's *not* my fault if you use it incorrectly, but if you follow instructions, it should work its magic and work it well. Come back in three nights' time and I'll have it for you." The Green Faerie shooed her away.

As Teran walked toward the door, her only thought was how she was going to explain this to January. She pushed open the greenhouse door and stared out into the windy night. The breeze swelled around her, and Teran had a premonition that something was on the way. Something that would connect itself to the ritual of the Green Faerie. What it was, Teran couldn't tell. All she did know was that she had just unleashed Pandora's box, and what was in it would only be revealed in time.

PLAYLIST

I often write to music, and WOODLAND WEB was no exception. However, I took an entirely different approach. I listened to a couple playlists on YouTube of music to focus by. The two channels I used were:

- **Meditative Mind** (you can buy their music on Amazon): Their Hang Drum and Tabla music
- **Chill Music Lab**

BIOGRAPHY

New York Times, *Publishers Weekly*, and *USA Today* bestselling author Yasmine Galenorn writes urban fantasy and paranormal romance, and is the author of over one hundred books, including the Wild Hunt Series, the Fury Unbound Series, the Bewitching Bedlam Series, the Indigo Court Series, and the Otherworld Series, among others. She's also written nonfiction metaphysical books. She is the 2011 Career Achievement Award Winner in Urban Fantasy, given by RT Magazine. Yasmine has been in the Craft since 1980, is a shamanic witch and High Priestess. She describes her life as a blend of teacups and tattoos. She lives in Kirkland, WA, with her husband Samwise and their cats. Yasmine can be reached via her website at **Galenorn.com**. You can find all her links at her **LinkTree**.

Indie Releases Currently Available:

Moonshadow Bay Series:
   Starlight Web
   Midnight Web

Conjure Web
Harvest Web
Shadow Web
Weaver's Web
Crystal Web
Witch's Web
Cursed Web
Solstice Web
Dreamer's Web
Woodland Web

Winter's Spell Trilogy:
Weaving Winter

Night Queen Series:
Tattered Thorns
Shattered Spells
Fractured Flowers

Starlight Hollow Series:
Starlight Hollow
Starlight Dreams
Starlight Demons
Starlight Witch

Magic Happens Series:
Shadow Magic
Charmed to Death

Hedge Dragon Series:
The Poisoned Forest
The Tangled Sky

The Wild Hunt Series:

The Silver Stag
Oak & Thorns
Iron Bones
A Shadow of Crows
The Hallowed Hunt
The Silver Mist
Witching Hour
Witching Bones
A Sacred Magic
The Eternal Return
Sun Broken
Witching Moon
Autumn's Bane
Witching Time
Hunter's Moon
Witching Fire
Veil of Stars
Antlered Crown

Lily Bound Series
    Soul jacker

Chintz 'n China Series:
    Ghost of a Chance
    Legend of the Jade Dragon
    Murder Under a Mystic Moon
    A Harvest of Bones
    One Hex of a Wedding
    Holiday Spirits
    Well of Secrets
    Chintz 'n China Books, 1 – 3: Ghost of a Chance,
Legend of the Jade Dragon, Murder Under A
Mystic Moon
    Chintz 'n China Books, 4-6: A Harvest of Bones,

One Hex of a Wedding, Holiday Spirits

Whisper Hollow Series:
    Autumn Thorns
    Shadow Silence
    The Phantom Queen

Bewitching Bedlam Series:
    Bewitching Bedlam
    Maudlin's Mayhem
    Siren's Song
    Witches Wild
    Casting Curses
    Demon's Delight
    Bedlam Calling: A Bewitching Bedlam Anthology
    Wish Factor (a prequel short story)
    Blood Music (a prequel novella)
    Blood Vengeance (a Bewitching Bedlam novella)
    Tiger Tails (a Bewitching Bedlam novella)

Fury Unbound Series:
    Fury Rising
    Fury's Magic
    Fury Awakened
    Fury Calling
    Fury's Mantle

Indigo Court Series:
    Night Myst
    Night Veil
    Night Seeker
    Night Vision
    Night's End
    Night Shivers

Indigo Court Books, 1-3: Night Myst, Night Veil, Night Seeker (Boxed Set)

Indigo Court Books, 4-6: Night Vision, Night's End, Night Shivers (Boxed Set)

Otherworld Series:
    Moon Shimmers
    Harvest Song
    Blood Bonds
    Otherworld Tales: Volume 1
    Otherworld Tales: Volume 2
For the rest of the Otherworld Series, see website at **Galenorn.com.**

Bath and Body Series (originally under the name India Ink):
    Scent to Her Grave
    A Blush With Death
    Glossed and Found

Misc. Short Stories/Anthologies:
    The Longest Night (A Pagan Romance Novella)

Magickal Nonfiction: A Witch's Guide Series.
    Embracing the Moon
    Tarot Journeys
    Totem Magick

39399986R00061